TO CHERISH

THE MCNALLYS

LAURA SCOTT

READSCAPE PUBLISHING, LLC

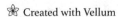

Jemma McNally kneaded a lump of dough while her three-and-a-half-year-old son Trey played with his miniature race cars in the living room. The lapping sound of waves hitting the rocky shore of Lake Michigan were audible through the French doors she'd opened to let in the balmy May breeze.

She put a little more muscle into the dough, determined to push her worrisome thoughts aside to focus on recreating her grandma's Irish brown bread recipe from memory. She wanted to try it out before their first guests arrived the upcoming weekend. She and her twin sister, Jazzlyn, were holding the grand opening of The McNallys' B&B this upcoming Friday. Frankly, her stomach was knotted up at the thought of feeding a house full of strangers.

Cooking had always relaxed her, until now. Turning her hobby into a business was intimidating to say the least. Especially since her ex-husband hadn't wanted her to work outside the home. After leaving him, she'd gone back to teaching, but this was a whole new adventure. Her experience in running a business was non-existent. And even after being divorced from her ex-husband, she could still hear Randal's voice in a tiny corner of her mind telling her she was stupid and useless.

"Daddy!"

Her son's voice sliced through her like a knife. Yanking her hands from the dough, Jemma frantically raced into the living room, her gaze sweeping the area for any sign of her abusive ex-husband.

"Trey?" Her gaze landed on the open French door, and she immediately rushed outside.

Her three-year-old son was scurrying toward the gazebo on chubby legs. She caught a flash of something dark in the corner of her eye, but she didn't dare take her gaze off her son. Running as if her life depended on it, because it did, she caught up with her son, scooping the boy into her arms and clutching him tightly.

"Where?" Her voice was little more than a hoarse croak. Hunching her shoulders, bracing for a possible physical attack, she looked around the backyard. "Where's Daddy?"

"There." Trey pointed a stubby finger toward the lake. Off in the distance she could see a sailboat, but nothing else. She turned in a full circle, searching the entire area.

But there was nothing. No sign of the ex-husband she'd driven over a hundred miles from Bloomington, Illinois, to McNally Bay, Michigan, to escape.

A hundred and twenty miles and two state lines that didn't seem nearly far enough.

Feeling vulnerable out in the open, even late in the morning on a bright May day, she whirled around and carried Trey inside the B&B, this time closing the French doors behind her. After setting Trey back on his feet, she made sure the doors were locked, willing her thundering heartbeat to return to normal.

There was no proof that Randal had been out there. She could have imagined seeing something out of the corner of her eye. And maybe Trey had mistaken the sailboat out on Lake Michigan for the old fishing boat her ex owned.

But fear gnawed at her. For a moment, she considered calling her twin. Jazz was working with her fiancé, Dalton on renovating his recent home purchase located right next door. She pulled out her phone but then realized it was better to go straight to the police. She had a current restraining order against Randal, and if by some freak chance he'd actually enticed her son to go outside in an effort to kidnap him, she needed to notify the authorities.

At least she knew the Clark County Sheriff's Deputies weren't on a first-name basis with her ex, the way half the Bloomington Police Department was.

Ignoring the sticky bits of dough clinging to her trembling fingers, she made the call. The dispatchers voice was calm and soothing. "Clark County Sheriff's Department, what's the nature of your emergency?"

"I believe my ex-husband has violated the restraining order I have against him. I'd like to file a formal complaint."

"Are you safe?" the dispatcher asked.

Jemma grimly wondered if she'd ever feel safe, again. "I think so. I don't see anyone lurking outside, but I think he's been here. I'm at The McNally B and B."

"I'll send a deputy."

"Thank you." Jemma disconnected from the call, then made her way back into the kitchen to wash her hands and wipe down her phone. She placed a damp towel over the dough, then began to pace, wondering how long it would take the deputy to arrive.

She knew that Randal could find her here easily enough, considering McNally Bay had been named after her great-grandparents who had immigrated from Ireland during the potato famine. She'd hoped and prayed that time and distance would work in her favor, but apparently not.

Silently ruing the day she'd met Randal Cunningham, much less married him, she pivoted and paced the opposite direction.

"Look, Mommy!" Trey held up a small car in his chubby hand. "A police car!"

She forced herself to smile at her son, hoping he wasn't picking up on her distress. "It's great, sweetie. Do you have a fire truck, too?"

He nodded and searched his miniature cars until he found the fire truck. "Here, Mommy." He pushed it into her hand. "For you. Play wif me?"

"Sure." She dropped to the floor beside him, crossing her legs into the lotus position. She hadn't practiced any yoga since moving to McNally Bay, but maybe it was time to get back to it.

Heaven knew, she could use something to help her relax. This constant living in fear wasn't healthy.

For her or for Trey.

Ten minutes later, she heard the sound of a car engine. She stood and pulled a knife from the large butcher block before cautiously approaching the front door.

She doubted Randal would be so stupid as to boldly approach the house, but she wasn't about to take any chances.

A brown sedan pulled to a stop in front of the B&B, the words Clark County Sheriff's Department stenciled along the side. Breathing out a sigh of relief, she quickly opened the door.

She inwardly groaned when Deputy Garth Lewis slid out from behind the wheel. Oh, he was nice enough, but he was also tall, with short dark hair and bright blue eyes, and far too attractive for his own good. This wasn't the first time she'd met him; he'd come to the house a few weeks ago when her sister had been almost killed by her ex-fiancé.

As a cop, he was the last man on the planet she'd be interested in. Especially if she were open to entering into a relationship at all, which she wasn't. Bad enough that her one monumental mistake had nearly cost her everything she held dear, she wasn't going to even consider going down that path again.

Especially not with a cop.

"Deputy," she greeted him politely as he stepped into the great room. Next to the kitchen, she loved her grand-parents' great room, with its cathedral ceiling, massive stone fireplace, Cliffs of Moher oil painting above the mantel, and the dark cherry antique furniture. She hadn't made it to the attic yet to find the silver candlesticks she was certain were packed away up there. "Thanks for coming."

"That's my job." He eyed the knife she still held in her hand warily. "What happened? The dispatcher said no one was hurt."

She flushed, feeling foolish for grabbing the knife. Turning on her heel, she headed back into the kitchen to put it away, then wiped the damp palms of her hands against her soft denim jeans.

"It's probably nothing—," she began, but was interrupted by her son.

"Policeman!" Trey's young voice held excitement, and she was upset to find her son approaching the deputy without an ounce of fear. "You're a policeman!"

"I sure am." Deputy Lewis swept a glance over the area, as if making sure there were no threats, before dropping to one knee so he wasn't looming over her son. "I see you have a police car in your hand there, too."

"Vroom," Trey said, waving the car around. "Do you got one like this?"

"Not exactly. Mine is brown, matches my uniform, see?"

Trey nodded curiously, then reached out to touch his badge. "Mine."

"No, it's not yours, honey." Jemma quickly came to her senses and crossed over to pull Trey's hand away from the deputy's badge. Despite what she'd gone through with Randal, it appeared Trey still idolized the police.

It wasn't his fault, she'd worked hard to make sure her son wasn't afraid of the authorities. Still, the possibility of Randal showing up in his uniform to secretly snatch Trey away haunted her.

Trey's lower lip trembled. "But I wanna badge . . ."

"How about this one?"

Jemma was surprised when Deputy Lewis pulled a shiny plastic badge out of his pocket. Her son's eyes lit up with delight.

"Thanks, policeman!"

Crisis averted for the moment, Jemma watched as Deputy Lewis clipped the toy badge to Trey's T-shirt. Her son began to strut around the living room, with his chest thrust out. "I'm the police," he announced with glee.

"You sure are," Deputy Lewis agreed as he stood. He glanced at Jemma with a rueful smile. "Hope you don't mind."

"Of course not." Her voice sounded strained, even to her own ears. She tried to shake it off. "Would you like a cup of coffee?"

"That would be great, thanks."

She poured him a mug from the pot she'd recently

brewed for her twin sister, Jazz who adored coffee. Jemma preferred tea, and added more hot water to her own mug while trying to wrestle her rioting emotions under control. She didn't want to break down in front of the deputy, but the small act of kindness he'd shown her son had only highlighted the lack of a father figure in Trey's life.

All because she'd made the wrong choice in choosing Randal as a husband. Because she'd fallen for his lies. Because she hadn't escaped, sooner.

And now lived in fear of losing Trey, forever.

GARTH FOLLOWED Jemma into the kitchen, the scent of yeast making his stomach rumble.

"Cream and sugar?" She glanced at him over her shoulder.

"Black is fine."

She handed him the mug, and he did his best to ignore the tingle of awareness he felt as her fingers brushed his. Idiot. He gave himself a mental head-slap. She was a woman in trouble, not a potential date. Granted, he didn't see any obvious threat when he'd done a quick sweep of the area upon arrival, but that didn't mean there wasn't someone hiding out of sight.

"Thanks." He took a sip, eyeing her over the rim. She looked too young to have a son, with her deep brown eyes and blond hair pulled back into a ponytail. He knew she was Jazz's twin sister, but they were complete opposites when it came to their features. Jazz had dark hair and green eyes, compared to Jemma's blond hair and deep brown eyes. There was a streak of flour along her cheek, and he had to restrain himself from reaching up to wipe it away. He cleared his throat. "Why don't you take a seat and start at the beginning?"

As suddenly exhausted, she dropped into the closest chair. "It's probably nothing . . ."

"You brought a knife to the front door," he reminded her, wryly. That and the look of panic in her eyes had gotten to him in a big way. "It's not nothing. Go on."

She blew out a breath, a steely resolve in her gaze. "I have a restraining order against my ex-husband, Randal Cunningham. He lives and works in Bloomington, Illinois, as a cop."

A cop? What were the odds? He winced. "I see."

"I was awarded sole custody because of a domestic dispute that turned violent." She dropped her gaze, as if unable to bear looking at him. "At the time, Randal didn't put up a fuss, no doubt because he wanted to keep his job. But that was nine months ago, and recently, he's told me he wants to go back to court to sue for joint custody of Trey."

Garth jotted down her ex-husband's name so he could pull up the court order. "What happened this morning?"

"I heard Trey call, *Daddy,* and when I rushed in, he was outside walking toward the gazebo. I ran out to pick him up and asked him where he saw Daddy, and he pointed to the sailboat on the lake."

"A sailboat?" he echoed in confusion.

She nodded, staring down at her lap, where her fingers were twisted together. "My ex owns a fishing boat. I know Trey is only three and a half and could be confused about what he saw, but I want this incident on record, just in case Randal was here." She finally lifted her gaze to his. "I can't risk my ex-husband taking Trey away from me."

Garth understood her concern but also knew there wasn't much to work with. A three-and-a-half-year-old pointing at a sailboat on the lake and saying the word daddy wasn't exactly a compelling argument that her ex had shown up here, violating the restraining order. "Have you noticed anything else?"

"I thought I saw something dark out of the corner of my eye, but when I picked up Trey and looked around, I didn't see anyone." Her gaze held dull resignation. "I told you it was probably nothing."

Yet that nothing had caused her to pick up a butcher knife before coming to the door. The idea of her ex-husband physically abusing her made him feel sick to his stomach. He'd been involved in several domestic incidents. In his opinion, they were the most dangerous call a cop could respond to. Emotions always ran high and spouses or partners often acted out irrationally.

"Hey, it's a good thing to have this complaint on record," he said, even though he knew it wouldn't go anywhere. "When's the last time you've seen Randal?"

She shook her head. "Months. I spoke to him two months ago, that's when he threatened to sue for joint custody." She hesitated, then shrugged. "There was an incident at Trey's preschool a few weeks ago in April, where a man showed up claiming to be his father to pick him up for a doctor's appointment. Thankfully, the teacher said she had to verify with me first, so the guy left."

The close call made the back of his neck tingle. "Was she able to identify him as Cunningham?"

"No. She described a thin man with dirty-blond hair." Her tortured gaze locked on his. "Randal is big, built like a defensive lineman, not as much fat as muscle. He has black hair and used to have a black goatee. He may have shaved his face, but it still wouldn't change the rest of his appearance, much."

"That's odd," he muttered. "Unless Randal hired the guy?"

"That's what I suggested, but the police claimed there was no proof." Jemma sighed. "You need to know that a lot of the Bloomington cops believe the lies Randal tells them about me. They think I'm making all this up in an attempt to hurt Randal because of the divorce, as if he was the one who'd filed." There was a hint of bitterness in her tone.

"I'm sorry," he said, feeling helpless.

"Thanks, but it doesn't matter. That incident was the impetus I needed to send me packing up my stuff and making the move here to McNally Bay." Her attempt to smile was a bit pathetic, but he gave her points for trying.

Garth stared at the guy's name on his notepad realizing that it wouldn't be difficult to find Jemma McNally here at her grandparents' mansion. The whole town was named after them.

He didn't like thinking about her ex-husband showing up here, trying to get to his son. The boy was innocent in all this and was clearly a friendly kid.

One who didn't seem to be afraid of his father.

Was Cunningham, right? Was Jemma stretching the truth to keep her son?

She didn't seem like the type to do that. And she had picked up a butcher knife. He scowled and tightened his grip on his stubby pencil, not liking the situation one bit.

"Please." Jemma's soft voice pulled him from his thoughts. "I need you to believe me. I need you to believe that Randal is capable of kidnapping his own son, and worse."

"I'll make the report," he said, not ready to admit whether or not he believed her. "I'll also ensure that all the deputies have a picture of your ex-husband in their vehicles. If he shows his face, we'll find him."

"Thank you." Jemma's tentative smile transformed her sweet features into stunning beauty. When she reached over to rest her hand on his arm, every muscle in his body went tense.

She quickly pulled her hand away, as if she'd surprised herself with the gesture. He hastily swallowed the last of his coffee and stood, anxious to get out of there. He couldn't afford to let his attraction for Jemma get in the way of doing his job.

That had happened once before with disastrous results. Kate's face and that of her four-year-old daughter, Sophie, flashed in his mind for a moment, before he ruthlessly shoved it away.

No way. Uh-uh. Wasn't happening.

He couldn't, wouldn't go down that painful path again.

Jemma and her adorable son were better off remaining distant acquaintances that he needed to protect.

He absolutely refused to open himself up to more heartache.

2

"I'll take another look around outside," Deputy Lewis said abruptly. He set his coffee cup aside and strode through the living room, heading out through the French doors. Jemma sat for a moment, trying not to think about how empty the house felt without the deputy being there.

Soon enough, the place wouldn't be empty at all. They'd have guests staying there, too. At least on the weekends, when the majority of their reservations happened to be.

She turned her attention to the Irish brown bread, but her heart wasn't in it. The very thought of Randal being anywhere near McNally Bay rattled her.

Her ex-husband was capable of just about anything. And the fact that she'd managed to escape him seemed to have added fuel to the fire. It was as if he'd become obsessed with her.

And Trey.

When her phone rang, she startled so badly, she knocked her elbow sharply on the edge of the counter. Wincing at the pain zinging down her arm, she told herself to get a grip as she answered Jazz's call. "Hey, how's demolition going?"

"Great, but what's up?"

Jemma frowned, wondering if her twin was experiencing another premonition. Once she'd assumed the shared empathy twins felt for each other was nothing but hooey, until the night Randal had attacked her. Jazz had called her from Chicago, instinctively knowing something was amiss.

She forced lightness in her tone. "What do you mean? Nothing is up."

"Then why is there a Sheriff's Deputy over there?"

Jemma let out her breath in a soundless sigh. She should have figured either Jazz or Dalton would see the squad car in the driveway from their neighboring property to the west. "Oh, it's fine. Just my overactive imagination."

"Randal?"

"Trey called out the word daddy and I freaked out," she finally admitted. "But when I asked where Daddy was, he pointed to a sailboat out on the lake, so I figure he must have gotten confused."

"I'll be there in two minutes."

"No! Don't be ridiculous. I told you it's nothing. Deputy Lewis has already taken my statement and is right now looking around outside. There's nothing you can do here."

Jazz didn't say anything for a long moment. "The other reason I called is because we're breaking for lunch. Dalton is picking up pizza. We'll bring it over and share with you and Trey, okay?"

She normally made pizza from scratch but wasn't up to that task at the moment. "Sounds good."

"See you soon."

"Okay." Jemma disconnected from the call, wishing she

wasn't such a burden to her twin. Over the past few weeks, she'd done nothing but lean on Jazz for support.

There were times she wished Randal would violate his restraining order, just so that he'd be arrested. Maybe then he'd leave her and Trey alone.

She forced herself to finish the dough, then placed it in the bread maker. Not exactly the way Grandma used to make it, since they didn't have bread makers back in Grandma's day, but she didn't care. Her guests probably wouldn't know the difference.

Besides, the charm of baking like her grandma had worn off.

Ten minutes later, Deputy Lewis returned, his expression thoughtful. She noticed he carried a clear plastic bag holding a small square card inside. Her blood went cold.

"Does Trey have baseball cards?" He held it up for her to see.

A wave of dizziness washed over her, as if all the oxygen had been sucked from the room. "Not here," she finally managed.

Deputy Lewis frowned. "This isn't Trey's?"

She dropped into a chair, her thoughts whirling. She hadn't seen the pack of baseball cards that Randal had collected for Trey since the night of the attack nine months ago. After the assault, Jazz had come to get her and Trey, they'd gone straight to the police and from there into a safe house. All the toys Trey currently had here at the B&B, including the miniature cars, she'd bought herself.

She hadn't purchased any baseball cards. For one thing, Trey was too young for them, but more so because that night she'd barely escaped, Randal had threatened to bash her head in with his baseball bat.

Her husband was into baseball. A big Cubs fan. And he

played on the Bloomington baseball team.

"Jemma?" Deputy Lewis moved closer, his clear blue eyes full of concern.

She did her best to pull herself together. "I—um, can I take a closer look at it?"

"Sure." He handed over the plastic bag.

Her stomach twisted into knots when she saw the card was that of Anthony Rizzo, one of the star hitters for the Cubs. She dragged her gaze up to the deputy. "It's Randal's."

He lifted a skeptical brow. "Your ex-husband collects baseball cards?"

"My ex-husband is a Cubs fan, and yes, he collected baseball cards, supposedly for Trey," she said in a dull voice. "I know he left the card behind on purpose."

"It could have been left by some kids," Deputy Lewis pointed out.

A flash of anger had her leaping to her feet. "What kind of cop are you?" she demanded. "We're five miles out of town with no other kids around, and it rained last evening. How would a kid get out here without anyone seeing him? If a kid had left that card behind a few days ago, it would be a soggy mess."

"Yes, I'm aware of when it last rained." Deputy Lewis tugged the bag from her fingers and slipped it into his pocket. "I'll see if we can lift any fingerprints."

"He's too smart for that," Jemma said, her burst of anger fading to a dull resignation. "I told you he's a cop."

"Anyone can make a mistake."

Not Randal. Not over something as basic as fingerprints. Leaving the card behind hadn't been a mistake either.

He'd done it on purpose. His way of telling her he knew where she and Trey were living. Subtle cruelty was Randal's specialty.

This was all likely part of his master plan. To make her look foolish, or worse, crazy.

She felt sick to her stomach. Randal would certainly get sole custody of Trey if she was deemed incapable of caring for her son due to mental disease or defect.

She couldn't lose Trey. Randal didn't want his son. Hadn't really paid much attention to him while they were together.

All Randal wanted was for her to suffer.

And she secretly feared he wouldn't hesitate to do something to Trey as a way to hurt her.

GARTH HATED SEEING the stark despair on Jemma's face but was helpless as to what he could do or say to make her feel better.

The baseball card alone wasn't proof that Cunningham had violated his restraining order. But knowing the jerk was a cop who'd already attacked her once made him think that the card hadn't been left by accident.

Jemma's ex could very well be stalking her. He felt bad for doubting her.

"I want you to take my personal number," he said abruptly. "You can call me at any time, even if I'm off duty."

Jemma looked surprised, then doubtful. "I'm sure it's not necessary for you to be on call for me twenty-four/seven."

"Please."

She hesitated, then nodded. She pulled out her cell phone and punched in his number. When she finished, she looked up at him and they locked gazes for several moments.

"Lunchtime!" Jazz's cheerful voice broke the silence.

Jemma's twin carried in two boxes of pizza followed by her twin's fiancé, Dalton O'Brien, who carried a gallon container of some sort of soft drink.

Spicy tomato and pepperoni intermingled with the scent of homemade bread. His mouth watered as his stomach rumbled, but he told himself it was time to go.

"Hey, Garth, why don't you join us for lunch?" Dalton asked. "We've got more than enough food, here."

"Oh, I really shouldn't . . ." he began, but Jazz was already nodding in agreement.

"You must get time to eat, don't you?" Jazz asked. "Even on duty?"

"Well, yeah, but . . ."

"Come on, sit down and take a break," Dalton urged.

All efforts to leave were derailed when Trey came running into the kitchen, the plastic badge still prominently displayed on his small chest. "We're both policemans, right?"

"Policemen," Jemma corrected, scooping her son up into her arms and cuddling him close. The boy had the same blond hair and dark eyes as his mother, and Garth felt a pang near the center of his heart at the thought of Cunningham getting anywhere close to them.

Jazz opened the pizza boxes, and Dalton pulled plates and glasses out of the cupboard, including a setting for him. Garth knew he shouldn't stay but somehow couldn't dredge up the will to go.

"You're sure there's enough?"

"There's plenty," Jemma said reassuringly, favoring him with a hesitant smile. Trey wiggled in her arms, so she reluctantly set him on the floor. "Come on, Trey, we need to wash up."

"Nooo." Trey seemed to share every kid's aversion to soap and water. "Don't wanna wash up."

"All policemen wash their hands before eating," Garth pointed out.

Trey eyed him suspiciously. "They do?"

"Yes. Always. Would you like it if we washed our hands together?"

"Okay," Trey agreed.

"Thanks, Deputy Lewis," Jemma said in a low voice, as they worked together to hold Trey up so he could wash his hands in the sink. Jemma grabbed a towel to dry her son's hands, then stepped back.

"Call me Garth," he said, gently setting Trey back on his feet.

She hesitated, then nodded. "Okay, first names it is."

He felt ridiculously pleased by her acquiescence. Not that it should matter to him one way or the other what she called him.

The impromptu pizza party was nice, and he found himself enjoying the banter between Dalton and the twin sisters. He knew that Dalton and Jazz were renovating the old Stevenson house located next door, Dalton's recent purchase. Apparently, there was an ongoing music war between country and eighties rock bands while Jazz and Dalton worked.

He suspected Jazz and her taste for eighties rock was winning the music war.

By the time they were finished eating and drinking lemonade, Trey's face and hands were liberally smeared with tomato sauce. There was even some matted in the boy's hair.

A timer went off, sending Jemma surging to her feet. "My bread!" She opened a boxlike device and then lifted a loaf of homemade brown bread out. Even though he was stuffed from the pizza, he wouldn't have minded sampling the homemade bread.

Jemma glanced over at him, as if sensing his thoughts. A smile tugged at the corner of her mouth. "I need all of you to be taste testers to let me know if this is good enough to serve our first guests this weekend."

"Twist my arm," Garth joked. "I've been dying to try a slice since I walked in."

"Really?" Jemma's cheeks were pink, probably from the warmth of the bread. She pulled a ridged knife from the butcher block and began to slice. She put the bread on a small plate and set it in front of him, along with some butter. "You're first up, then."

The bread was warm enough to melt the butter into an oozing softness. He took a bite and tried not to moan with pleasure. "It's amazing," he managed. "You're an incredible cook, Jemma."

"Thanks, but this is my grandma's recipe," Jemma said. "She was the true mastermind of the kitchen."

"Don't be modest, Jem," Jazz said, having tasted her own sample. "Grandma may have taught you many of her Irish baking secrets, but you still have talent. Trust me, our guests are going to love anything you make for them."

"I'd pay to stay here just for the bread," Garth agreed. Then realized how that sounded and tried to backpedal. "I mean, your guests will appreciate every slice. Your business will skyrocket once the word gets out about your bread."

"Okay, enough," Jemma protested with a small laugh. "You've convinced me already. No need to go overboard with your praise."

Jemma was beautiful when she smiled, and Garth had to force himself to tear his gaze away.

What was he doing here? First giving her his private cell number, then offering his first name. If he didn't watch out, he'd repeat his mistakes of the past.

His radio went off, and he quickly stood and turned away to respond to the call. "This is unit ten."

"Unit ten, there's a D and D out at the Pine Cone Campsite," the dispatcher said. "Patrons are requesting a response."

Drunk and disorderly, he thought with a grimace. These types of calls generally came in at bar time, not at quarter to one on a Monday afternoon. "Unit ten, responding." He turned and raked his gaze over the group at the table. "Sorry to eat and run, but I have to go. Thanks for the lunch and the homemade bread."

"Anytime," Dalton said.

Jemma followed him through the great room to the front door. "Take care, Garth. Be safe."

"I will." He glanced at her. "I'll be in touch if we find anything on the baseball card."

She nodded but didn't respond, and he knew she didn't harbor any false hopes. Leaving her standing in the doorway as he walked to his squad car wasn't easy. Every nerve in his body longed to stay near her side. To protect her, and maybe because he was drawn to the sense of home and family she represented.

But he slid behind the wheel and quickly made a circle in the wide driveway, before heading out to the highway. When he hit the highway, he flipped on his lights and sirens.

He made good time covering the ten miles between the B&B and the Pine Cone Campsite. When he arrived, there was a man stumbling around with a bottle of Wild Turkey Whiskey in his hand, occasionally tipping the bottle to his mouth and taking a sip.

"I'm a good father," he shouted, even though the other campers had made themselves scarce. He could see a man and woman huddled behind a tree near a small camper and figured they were the ones who'd made the call. "No one has the right to take my son away from me."

The guy didn't appear to be armed, so Garth decided not to call for backup just yet. He got out from behind the wheel and lightly rested his hand on the butt of his gun as he warily approached the drunken camper. The way the guy was railing on about fatherhood made him wonder if this could possibly be Jemma's ex-husband.

"Put down the bottle, sir, and place both of your hands on your head," he said in a deep authoritative tone.

"Who are you?" The guy slurred his words and blinked as if he couldn't focus. The drunk staggered, then lifted the bottle to take another slurp. "Whatdayawant?"

"I'm Deputy Lewis," Garth responded. "And I want you to put down the bottle, right now. I need you to place your hands on your head so no one gets hurt. Understand?"

"I didn't do nuthin' illegal," the man protested. He took another staggering step toward Garth, then tripped over a rock and fell forward, hitting the ground face first. The bottle of Wild Turkey went flying, trickling booze all over the place.

Garth instantly moved in, jamming his knee in the center of the guy's back and holding his head to the ground with one hand as he used the other to pat him down, searching for a weapon. There was a penknife in the right front pocket of the guy's jeans, but thankfully, nothing more lethal.

The drunk man began to struggle. "Hey! Lemme up! I didn't do nothin' illegal!"

Garth leaned all his weight on the guy's back as he

wrenched both wrists back to cuff him. The awful scent of sweat and alcohol oozed from the guy's pores. Once he had the guy secured, he eased up and rose to his feet. The drunk kicked at Garth but missed by a mile. With a sigh, Garth hauled the guy upward and half-walked, half-dragged him toward the squad car.

"You're under arrest for disorderly conduct," he said, pressing the man against the side of the vehicle. He pulled out the penknife first, then the man's wallet. His heart thumped with anticipation as he opened the worn leather and looked at his ID.

The driver's license was from Illinois, but it identified the man as Stephan Ahern. Not Randal Cunningham. He stared at the photo, the image not exactly a recent replication of the guy he currently held pressed against the squad car.

And it was freaky that the guy's address was Bloomington, Illinois, the same place Jemma McNally had lived. The same city where Randal Cunningham was a cop.

Sure, it was a big city, but what were the odds they'd both end up in Clark County?

"What's your name?" Garth demanded, wondering if the driver's license was forged.

"Steve. So, what? I'm not allowed to drink at my own campsite?" Ahern's drunk tone turned whiny. "Hey, I got rights."

"Yeah, you have the right to remain silent, anything you say can and will be used against you in a court of law." Garth continued reading Ahern his rights, wondering where this guy's wife/girlfriend and son were.

Hopefully, somewhere safe.

It would have been too easy to stumble upon Cunningham so soon after finding the baseball card.

Besides, Ahern had clearly been drinking since the moment he'd crawled out of his tent.

Garth glanced around the campsite, noticing how the one couple still remained huddled behind the tree, apparently still not feeling safe. Another deputy vehicle pulled up beside him, and Deputy Trina Waldorf slid out from behind the wheel. She helped Garth wrestle the drunken camper into the back seat.

"His name is Stephan Ahern, and he's from Bloomington, Illinois. He was rambling on about someone taking his son away when I pulled up," Garth said. "I need to do a background check on him, see if he has other outstanding warrants."

Trina nodded. "I'll run him for you," she offered.

"Yeah, okay," he agreed. "Let me know if you come up with something."

He drove Ahern to headquarters and booked him for disorderly conduct. When he finished tossing the guy in jail, Trina called.

"No outstanding warrants," Trina said. "But he does have a wife Amy and a seven-year old son, Daniel. And they have a no contact order against him."

"Thanks, Trina." He disconnected from the call. He didn't like that Ahern's situation was eerily similar to Jemma's.

Enough. He gave himself a mental shake. He was beginning to become too entangled in Jemma's and Trey's lives. As an officer of the law, it was his duty to keep them safe. Which meant he needed to maintain a healthy, professional distance from them. No more cozy meal sharing.

He knew better than most that getting personally involved was likely to get them both killed.

3

Jemma was preparing dinner, a shepherd's pie, another of her grandmother's Irish recipes, when she heard a car pull into the driveway. Wiping her hands on her grandma's old well-worn apron, decorated with tiny rosebuds and green vines that made her think of pictures she'd seen of Ireland, Jemma peered through the window in the front door.

Deputy Garth Lewis was back, and her heart gave an inappropriate thump of awareness when she saw him striding toward the door. Willing her ridiculous hormones away, she opened the door before he could knock. "Hi, Garth, come on in."

"Uh, no thanks." He looked ill at ease standing there. "I just need to ask you a couple of questions. Does the name Stephan Ahern mean anything to you?"

She felt the blood drain from her face and grasped the edge of the door to prevent herself from falling. "Yes. Why are you asking?"

Garth's eyebrows levered up as if he hadn't expected her answer. "How do you know him?"

She hesitated and glanced over her shoulder to make sure Trey was still preoccupied with his iPad computer game. She knew she had to limit her son's screen time, but it was a learning game recommended from his previous three-K program. Thankfully, he was entranced by the game and hadn't noticed Garth's arrival. "You better come in." She stepped back from the doorway.

Garth entered the house, bringing the scent of the woods with him. She figured it had to be his aftershave, because it was similar to what she'd smelled earlier. The scent was lethal to her ability to concentrate, so she attempted to put a bit of distance between them.

"I need to know about the connection you have with Ahern," he repeated, dropping into a seat across from her at the kitchen table.

She drew in a deep breath and nodded. "I used to teach second grade at Bloomington West Elementary. Mr. Ahern's son, Daniel, was one of my students."

Garth's expression was full of concern. "Go on."

"I noticed several bruises on the boy, particularly on his arms, and when I asked him what happened, he told me he fell."

"You didn't believe him."

She rolled her eyes. "Of course not. It was clear he was being hit at home, so I reported the parents to child protective services. They showed up at the house and heard Mr. Ahern yelling and the sound of a slap as they knocked at the door. They took Ahern into custody as it was clear he'd slapped his wife, and thankfully, Mrs. Ahern pressed charges and filed for divorce."

"Did Ahern know your husband?" Garth asked.

"I don't think so, why?" She frowned, trying to understand where he was going with all this.

"Ahern is in town, staying apparently at the Pine Cone Campsite roughly ten miles from here." Garth shrugged. "Seems like an odd coincidence."

For a moment, it felt as if the walls were closing in on her, and she struggled to suck in a breath to clear her head. "Yes, it is. Has he admitted to knowing Randal?"

"He's in no shape to admit to anything," Garth said with a wry grimace. "He blew a zero point two three on the breathalyzer we gave him just before we booked him for disorderly conduct. But I have him locked up and plan to question him further once he's sober."

Jemma wasn't surprised that Ahern was drunk, apparently that wasn't an uncommon occurrence for him. And being that drunk midday was indicative of a significant drinking problem. Regardless, the idea of Ahern being here in Clark County was disturbing.

What if the guy did know Randal? Was it possible the two were somehow working together against her? "Do you have a picture of him?" she abruptly asked. "I never met him personally; his wife was the one who regularly attended school functions."

Garth pulled a mug shot out of his pocket and handed it over. She stared at the slack-jawed man with bloodshot eyes and greasy dark hair. After a long moment, she handed the picture back. "He doesn't fit the description of the guy Trey's preschool teacher provided to the authorities who claimed to be there to take him to a doctor's appointment."

"Maybe, maybe not." Garth tucked the picture back into the breast pocket of his uniform. "Hair dye is cheap. Could be he used to be a dirty blond."

She shivered despite the warmth of the kitchen. Remembering how pathetic Ahern looked in his mug shot made her shake her head. "I don't know, it's hard to believe Randal would stoop so low as to hire this guy to take Trey."

Garth didn't say anything for a long minute. "I think it could be a cagey move on your ex's part," he argued softly. "The guy already has a reason to hold a grudge against you; he was ranting and raving about losing custody of his son when I arrived. Ahern could blame you for making the call to CPS."

She frowned. "But he's hardly reliable."

"The fact that the guy has a serious drinking problem provides additional coverage. Cunningham can argue that the guy was working alone, not by his direction, and who would believe a drunk over a Bloomington cop?"

Put that way, Jemma could admit he had a point. She knew firsthand how well cops stood up for other cops, regardless of the circumstances. The chill intensified, sinking deep into her bones. "Your theory could be right," she finally agreed. "I guess it's pretty obvious Randal would do just about anything to get what he wants."

Garth reached out to cup his hand over hers. "Try not to worry about it," he said in a soothing tone. "We have Ahern in custody, and I'm sure I can convince him to cooperate with the investigation."

She savored the warmth of Garth's hand on hers for a moment until she realized something. "If Ahern blew a zero point two three, then he couldn't have been the one who dropped the baseball card."

He gently squeezed her fingers, then removed his hand. The chill in her bones deepened as he nodded. "Maybe, maybe not. He could have come by earlier and dropped it. Why, I'm not sure. It also could be that Cunningham drove up here to meet with Ahern, found him drunk, so decided he was useless and came out here to get your son's attention and to plant the baseball card."

A sick feeling churned in her stomach. "Too bad we can't prove that. If we could, I'd have him arrested for violating his restraining order."

"I'll check the tolls, see if I can pick up his vehicle, but as you said, I doubt he'd use his own car to travel here and back. Too obvious."

Yeah, that was Randal all right. In her mind he was a snake, hiding and slithering around on the ground, stalking his prey before striking out with his poisoned fangs.

She hoped and prayed that Trey wasn't his intended victim. Better that Randal come after her, rather than their son. If anything happened to her, she felt certain Jazz would step in to raise Trey.

"Hey, it's okay." Garth apparently picked up on her distress. "We'll keep an eye out for Cunningham. If he's around, we'll find him."

She wanted desperately to believe him and forced a tight smile. "Thank you."

Their gazes locked and held for several moments. His eyes were the same blue as Lake Michigan outside the window, and she couldn't help being drawn to the shimmering depths.

But then he pulled his gaze away and abruptly jumped to his feet. "I have to finalize my report. Don't hesitate to call if you need anything."

"I won't." She followed him to the front door. "Thanks again."

He hesitated, glanced back at her, then nodded solemnly. "We're here to protect and serve our community."

The words were oddly stilted, and she frowned, but nodded. "I know."

"Take care of yourself and your son." He opened the door and left, not once looking back. She stood in the threshold, watching as he backed up, then drove away.

Randal hadn't held up his oath to protect and serve. He only cared about himself. She closed and locked the door, wishing for the zillionth time that she'd never accepted that first date or fallen for his fake charm.

Enough. Her life had taken this path for a reason, even if she couldn't quite figure out what it was. Hadn't that same thing happened to her twin? Jazz had found her fiancé kissing her bridesmaid the night of the rehearsal dinner and had immediately called off the wedding. Jazz had been devastated, but it turned out better for her twin in the end.

Jazz and Dalton were a great couple. A few weeks ago, Dalton had asked her to help him buy a ring. She and Jazz had different coloring but thankfully wore the same size clothes and the same ring size. She'd been thrilled to help. Now they were planning their wedding, trying to set a date in which all their brothers could attend.

Jemma was truly happy for her twin, but there were times when she caught the look of adoration pass between them that she couldn't prevent a prick of envy.

She'd wanted what they had. The same kind of love their parents and their grandparents and great-grandparents had shared.

Too bad, it wasn't meant to be.

Garth spent hours trying to verify the whereabouts of Randal Cunningham, and when the Bloomington, Illinois, PD Lieutenant Young had finally returned his call, Young claimed that Cunningham had been working the day shift starting at 0700 in the morning and finishing by 1530 in the afternoon. The lieutenant made it clear that Cunningham couldn't possibly have been anywhere near his ex-wife. Garth could tell by the way Young had sneered when he said the word *ex-wife*, that the lieutenant didn't respect Jemma one iota and probably didn't believe Cunningham had ever attacked her in the first place.

He thanked the lieutenant and hung up, inwardly marveling at Jemma's strength and determination to stand up for herself against at least a handful of cops within the Bloomington Police Department.

She'd said that many of them believed Cunningham's side of the story, and after a brief conversation with Lieutenant Young, he knew she was right. Good thing she had picked up her son and moved here to McNally Bay, Michigan.

The farther she stayed from Bloomington, Illinois, the better.

Before leaving for the day, Garth checked on Ahern. The guy was stretched out on his jail cell cot, snoring loud enough to rattle the ceiling tiles overhead. After making sure the deputy working the evening shift understood that Garth wanted to interrogate Ahern the following morning, he left.

His plan was to go to his apartment, but he somehow found himself driving past the McNally Mansion instead. He drove slowly, making sure to take note of any vehicles that might be lingering in the area.

It was a stretch to think that Lieutenant Young would risk his own career to cover a subordinate, yet he couldn't help wondering if the lieutenant had been truthful about Cunningham's whereabouts that day. After logging the baseball card in as evidence, he'd requested it to be checked for fingerprints. Unfortunately, as Jemma predicted, the tech hadn't found anything.

The card had been wiped clean, which was suspicious in and of itself. Any kid innocently losing a baseball card would have left at least one print if not more.

Garth parked off to the side of the road, just before the driveway leading to the McNally Mansion. Actually, it was now The McNallys' B&B, he thought with an odd sense of pride. He was happy to see the changes Jemma and Jazz had done to the place. As weird as it might sound, he'd thought the house looked lonely after the matriarch, Joan McNally, had passed away. Now that her grandchildren had returned to open a business, the place blossomed with life.

An added bonus was that he didn't have to chase away teenagers who'd sneaked onto the property to party on the weekends.

He sat in his car for almost five minutes, before shifting into gear and heading toward home. He rented a two-bedroom apartment near the center of town, with barely a sliver of a lakefront view. As he passed by Daisy's Diner, he decided to get a bite to eat.

The place was crowded, but the server, Ashley, waved him over to an empty stool at the counter. "Saved it just for you, Deputy Lewis."

"Thanks, Ash." He slid into the seat and glanced at the whiteboard listing of the specials. Sadly, this place was more of a home to him than his apartment. "I'll have the meatloaf and water, thanks."

"Sounds good." Ashley smiled again and moved away to place his order, returning a minute later with a glass of ice water.

He took a grateful gulp, then looked over at his fellow

diners. As a cop, he instinctively looked for any sign of trouble no matter if he was on or off duty.

Based on the number of strangers in the room, the warm May weather had caused an uptick in tourism in McNally Bay. He recognized a few of the regulars, Leon Tate and his daughter, Mary, were seated in one booth, the pair looking as cantankerous as usual. He'd questioned the old guy when Jazz had been having trouble with vandalism, but Tate hadn't admitted to anything, even though it was clear he didn't like the McNallys. The reason behind his dislike was still a mystery.

In contrast, he saw that Mrs. Betty Cromwell, one of the town's biggest gossips, was sitting in a booth across from Henry Banks, the town Mayor and recent widower. He grinned, wondering if she was hoping to become the new Mrs. Henry Banks.

The third woman he recognized in the diner was Carla Templeton and her eight-year-old daughter, Cassie. Carla worked at the grocery store and still lived with her mother, never once mentioning anything about the identity of Cassie's father. Not that he would normally care one way or the other, but he had heard the details from Mrs. Cromwell who had her nose in everyone's business.

There was no sign of Cunningham or anyone that he pegged as being sent by Jemma's ex. Sensing things were under control for the moment, he turned back around in time for Ashley to place a plate of meatloaf and steamed broccoli in front of him. "Here you go, Deputy."

"Thanks." He flashed an absent smile and dug into his meal. Ashley lingered at his side for a moment, and he glanced at her questioningly. She blushed and turned away.

The meatloaf wasn't bad, but it didn't hit the spot the way comfort food normally did. Up until now, he'd been more than satisfied with eating most of his meals at Daisy's Diner. But now he couldn't seem to get the scents of Jemma's cooking out of his mind. The bread had been amazing, and she'd been making something for dinner while he'd been there. The enticing scent of beef and veggies with a hint of garlic had made it difficult to concentrate as he'd asked her about a possible connection between her ex-husband and Ahern.

He'd been tempted to invite himself for dinner but managed to refrain. Although he suspected that if she'd offered for him to join them, he wouldn't have found the strength to decline.

Pathetic, he thought with a grimace. What was wrong with him? Why this sudden preoccupation with Jemma McNally? He gave himself a mental shake. He'd grown up in a series of foster homes, until he'd landed with a nice couple who helped him stay on the right path. His foster father, Doug Emory, had also been a cop, and Garth had quickly learned he couldn't sneak anything past the cagey guy. Oh, he'd tried, more than once, only to get caught every, single time. Susan Emory had never held those attempts against him either.

As a result of their acceptance of him the way he was, Garth had straightened up and managed to graduate high school, maybe not with honors but with a decent GPA. He then attended a two-year community college program to study criminal science. A degree he owed to the Emorys.

Doug had died shortly after he'd graduated from the academy from a massive heart attack, and Susan had followed a year later from cervical cancer. They hadn't formally adopted him, but the Emorys were the only parents he'd ever had. Seeing the way Jemma cared for Trey made him realize what he'd missed at that age. He only had vague memories of his mother using needles with strange men who always seemed to be coming and going. By the time he was five, he'd been removed from his mother's care and sent into his first foster home.

He'd learned his mother had died of a drug overdose just a year after he'd been taken away.

The Emorys had been great, and he owed them a lot. Although, he still often wondered about his birth mother and biological father. He told himself to let it go, to stop wallowing in the past. Garth finished his meatloaf, paid Ashley, and then made his way home. He did a load of laundry and tried to get lost in the baseball game, Detroit Tigers vs the Milwaukee Brewers, but it was a slow game with little action, and he gave up and went to bed.

But he didn't sleep.

At half past midnight, he gave up on that too and pulled on a comfy pair of jeans and a police academy sweatshirt. Then added his belt holster and weapon, just in case. He wanted to drive back to The McNallys' B&B to make sure everything remained quiet. He decided against using the squad car in favor of his personal black pick-up truck.

He tuned in a country rock station, silently agreeing with Dalton O'Brien's choice of music, as he drove out of town. The moon was shrouded in clouds making it difficult to see anything beyond the glare of his headlights.

Not that there was much to see, other than trees and shrubs. The McNallys' B&B was about six miles out of town, in a more rural part of Clark County.

Did he really expect Cunningham to make a move in kidnapping Trey in the middle of the night?

Doubtful.

Still, after everything that had transpired with Jazzlyn

and her former fiancé last month, he wasn't about to be lulled into complacency.

Garth parked along the side of the road again and slid out from behind the wheel. He'd walk the property line, and if he didn't see anything out of place, he'd head back to his apartment.

Trying once again to get some sleep.

The night air was cool, but he didn't mind. He silently made his way down the driveway toward the cheerful yellow mansion. The large three-car garage was located to the east, and remembering how he'd found the baseball card halfway between the house and the garage along the east side of the house, he decided to walk around that way first.

But he didn't find anything suspicious, including any indication someone else had been there recently. Not that it was easy to tell in the darkness. He rounded the garage, then paused for a moment, before crossing the stretch of lawn to the main house.

He stepped quietly, knowing the master suite where Jemma and Trey were staying was located along the east side of the house.

As he rounded the corner, his gaze rested momentarily on the glistening water of Lake Michigan. The McNally B&B offered an incredible view, and he knew that it would attract guests to the B&B.

A sudden movement from behind caught him off guard, and he attempted to lift his arm in a defensive move, mere seconds before something hard slammed against him. Pain reverberated along his upper arm and shoulder, ricocheting through his skull. He thought about Jemma and Trey, praying they were safe inside the master suite.

Then, there was nothing but darkness.

4

J emma sat up in bed, her eyes wide with alarm, when she heard a muffled thud somewhere outside. She pulled on a sweatshirt over her boxer shorts and T-shirt, grabbed her phone and tiptoed out of the bedroom, to avoid disturbing Trey.

The instant she shut the door behind her, she dialed 911. It seemed to take forever for the dispatcher to answer. "Clark County Sheriff's Department, what's your emergency?"

"I think there's someone outside my house." She kept her voice hushed as if whoever was outside might overhear. "Please send a deputy."

"Okay, ma'am. Stay inside with the doors locked, okay?"

"I will." She disconnected from the line and stood in the living room, soon to be dining area for their guests, staring out through the French doors, trying to see if anyone was out there.

She had a clear view all the way to the lake, although it wasn't easy to see in the darkness because the moon was covered by the clouds. She considered flipping on the outside lights but feared that might spook the intruder.

If it was Randal out there . . . she couldn't bear to finish the thought.

The silence was suffocating. Jemma tried to be strong, wanting, needing to maintain her independence, but couldn't seem to shake the fear that Randal was making his way toward the door right now.

She scrolled through her contacts to find Garth's number. Before she could talk herself out of it, she pressed the button to call him.

Within seconds she heard the faint sound of a phone ringing from the speaker she held to her ear as well as from outside. It took a minute for her to understand the implication. She crossed the room and pressed her face to the glass, peering into the darkness. This close to the window she could hear the ringing phone more distinctly.

She hit the stop button on her phone and instantly the ringing sound from outside ceased as well. Garth? Was he outside? Or just his phone? She stood frozen at the window, trying to summon the courage to go outside to see if Garth was in fact out there or not.

Not a good sign that he hadn't answered the phone. But what if he was hurt or worse? She'd hate herself if she didn't at least check.

Arming herself with a knife, she eased open one of the French doors and cautiously slid the screen aside. The sound of the screen door sliding along its tracks was incredibly loud in the absolute silence.

Her heart thundered in her chest. Every instinct told her to go back inside, but she stood where she was, convincing herself she could do this. She was smart and brave. She would not be a coward. Sucking in a breath, she slid through the narrow opening into the cool night. After crossing the concrete patio, her bare feet sank into soft, damp grass.

She moved silently toward the corner of the house, the spot from where she'd heard the ringing phone. A low groan reached her ears. Her heart lodged in her throat as she carefully peered around the corner.

At first, she didn't see anything, but then a dark shape and a flash of pale skin caught her eye. The lump on the ground moved again, and she finally realized that the man lying there was Garth.

She hurried forward, dropping to her knees beside him. "Garth? What happened? Are you okay?"

"Jemma?" His voice was low and husky. He winced and struggled to sit up. "Get back inside where it's safe."

There was a part of her that longed to do exactly that, but she forced herself to ignore it. "I've called nine one one, a deputy is on the way." She spoke in a loud tone, hoping that anyone lurking nearby would hear it.

"Good," he muttered. "But I still want you to go back inside."

Staring at his face in the moonlight, she could see a dark bruise marring his right temple. She set the knife down to free up her hands. "Come on, let's get you up to your feet. We'll go in, together."

He groaned and pushed himself up to his knees. Then he planted one hand against the side of the house, as if to steady himself. Placing her arm beneath his, she helped him stagger to his feet.

"Go inside," he said again, leaning heavily against the house. "I'll be right behind you."

"Together," she repeated, wrapping her arm around his waist for added support. "Ready?"

"Yeah."

With halting steps, they managed to get around to the corner to the French door that remained open. She mentally berated herself for being so stupid and hoped that no one had sneaked inside while she'd been with Garth.

She flipped on the lights and then helped Garth through the front living room to a kitchen chair. Once he was seated, she hurried back down the short hallway to the master suite, desperately needing to make sure Trey was still safe and asleep.

He was. Thank goodness. Her shoulders slumped in relief. Whoever had hit Garth must be long gone.

She hoped.

Closing the door of the master suite behind her, she returned to the kitchen. Garth was still sitting in the chair, gingerly pressing his fingers to the bruise on his right temple. In the light, she could see some swelling about the size of a duck egg.

"We need ice for that." She opened the freezer and pulled out a handful of small rounded ice cubes. After wrapping them in a clean washcloth, she pressed it against the side of his head.

He let out a low hiss of pain, but then brought his hand up to the ice pack. "Thanks. That helps."

Before she could ask more about what had happened, the flash of headlights flickered through the window of the front door. "That must be the deputy."

"Great." Garth's tone was dour. "Now everyone will hear about how I allowed some jerk to get the drop on me."

"It could have happened to anyone," she protested as she walked through the great room to the front door. She was surprised to find a rather petite red-haired deputy climb out of the squad car.

"Thanks for coming so quickly," Jemma said as she opened the door.

"I'm Deputy Waldorf," the female officer said. "Just wanted you to know I'll be looking around outside."

"You may want to speak with Deputy Lewis, first," Jemma informed her. "Appears whoever was out there assaulted him."

"What?" Deputy Waldorf's eyes widened in surprise, and she quickly pushed past Jemma to enter the house. As if she'd been in there before, she headed through the great room and into the kitchen. "Garth? What on earth happened?"

"Trina," he acknowledged with a wince. "Keep your voice down a notch, my head is pounding."

"Sorry." Trina's expression was full of concern as she examined Garth's injury, and Jemma had to squelch a flash of jealousy. What difference did it make if Garth and Trina had a thing going? She wasn't interested in traipsing down the relationship path again.

Trey's health and well-being came first, followed by running a successful B&B. She needed to establish some independence. She'd started by returning to her career as a teacher and had now jumped into managing her own business.

A man would only get in the way.

"What happened?" Trina asked, planting her hands on her slim hips. "Why are you out here?"

Garth winced and glanced at Jemma for a moment before answering. "I couldn't sleep, so I decided to take a quick look around, make sure things were safe and secure."

"Apparently, they weren't," Trina muttered, and Jemma shivered, realizing that it was entirely possible that Randal had been outside somewhere.

"Yeah, well, I went around the garage first and didn't see anything. Then I came up along the east side of the house. I heard and felt someone behind me and brought my arm up to defend myself seconds before something blunt hit me."

Jemma sucked in a harsh breath. "A baseball bat?" she asked in a hoarse whisper.

"I don't think so," Garth said quickly. "My injury would be far worse if the weapon had been a baseball bat. And it felt short and blunt against my arm." His gaze dropped to the wide work belt around Trina's waist. He reached up and lightly touched the dangling baton. "More like that."

The blood drained from her face as she stared at the stout blunt police baton.

Randal had assaulted Garth. She knew, deep in her bones, there could be no other explanation.

What would have happened if Garth hadn't come out to check on her tonight?

She curled her fingers into helpless fists. With sick certainty, she knew the cruelty wouldn't stop until either Randal was locked up or she was dead.

Desperately fearing he'd succeed in making it the latter.

GARTH COULDN'T BELIEVE he'd been so stupid as to get smacked in the head by a police baton. He wasn't a rookie and had to silently acknowledge that his shortsighted stunt of coming out to the B&B alone while off duty could have ended much worse.

Idiot. He deserved to get smacked in the head.

"The guy who attacked you is a cop?" Trina asked, a hint of skepticism in her voice.

"My ex-husband, Randal, is a cop, yes," Jemma said, her

expression full of fear and regret. "I have reason to believe he's stalking me, waiting for a chance to grab our son."

Trina's eyes widened, and she glanced between him and Jemma. "Okay, I think I need to take a look around outside, before I take you to the hospital."

"Not alone," he protested. "There's a small wooded area between this place and the house to the east. He might still be hanging around. I'm not going to the hospital, I'm fine."

"I'm sure he's long gone by now," Trina said, waving a hand dismissively. "Don't worry, I'll take extra precautions. And yes, you are going to the hospital."

"No." Garth removed the ice pack from his temple and set it on the table. "If you won't call for backup, we'll go together."

The way Jemma twisted her hands together betrayed the extent of her anxiety. He'd noticed she'd done that yesterday the first time he'd responded to her call.

Two emergency calls in less than twenty-four hours. He was starting to believe she was right about her ex and understood they need to catch Cunningham in the act, and soon.

Ignoring the ferocious pounding in his head wasn't easy, but he accompanied Trina outside, both carrying large flashlights.

Of course, they found nothing, aside from the knife Jemma left behind. Not even another baseball card, as he'd half-expected.

Guess the thunk on his head had been enough for Cunningham, he thought wryly as they went back inside.

Jemma had brewed a pot of coffee while waiting, although in her hands she cradled a cup with a tea bag floating inside.

"I made decaf," she offered. "If you're interested."

"None for me, thanks," Trina said. "I need to get back out on the road. Garth, I noticed your truck parked along the side of the road."

"Yeah, what about it?"

"You shouldn't drive. In fact, I still think you should go to the hospital."

"Not happening. It's a measly bump on the head."

"Stubborn," Trina muttered. "Are you sure you don't want a lift?"

"I'm sure." He picked up the ice pack and pressed it against the lump on his temple. The coldness only numbed a fraction of the pain, but he was grateful for that much. "Why are you on duty anyway?" He belatedly realized she had been on first shift with him the day before.

"Nathan called in sick, so I'm pulling a double. I'm working with Alex."

He winced again, realizing he'd have to make sure to report to work in the morning to help cover her open shift. "Okay. Just make sure you and Alex take turns swinging by this place during the night."

Jemma walked Trina to the front door, returning a few minutes later. She sat down beside him, sipping her tea.

"I wish you'd consider going to the hospital."

"I'm fine," he repeated. "Honest."

Her gaze was skeptical. "Okay, would you be willing to stay here for the rest of the night?"

He lifted his eyebrow in surprise, glad that the small movement didn't add to his current pain level. "Um, yeah. If that would make you feel better. But I don't want to cause you extra work."

Jemma's smile was sad. "I don't think I'll sleep a wink if you leave. Now that Dalton and Jazz are engaged, they've been staying at their new place so we can rent out as many rooms as possible." Her fingers twisted as she looked at him. "I could ask them to come here, but I'd rather not disturb them."

Logically, he knew that she had plenty of rooms available, at least until their first guests arrived. "I don't mind."

"Thank you." Jemma took another sip of her tea and then rose to her feet. "You can choose whichever room you like; there are seven of them upstairs, each with their own bathroom."

Personally, he didn't care either way. One room was much like the other. "Which is your favorite?"

"The yellow room," she answered without hesitation. "Jazz always preferred the green room, which was good because I called dibs on the yellow room when we came to visit Grandma and Grandpa. Sometimes had to share a room, though, and in those cases, we took turns."

Her eyes softened when she talked about her siblings, especially her twin. He couldn't imagine what it must have been like for her to grow up with loving parents and older siblings. His childhood had been as different from hers as salt and pepper. "Yellow room it is."

"Great. Do you need help navigating the stairs?"

"No." The word came out more forcefully than he intended. "Go back to bed, try to get some sleep, okay?"

"Okay." She carried her empty mug of tea to the sink, then turned back to face him. "Good night, Garth."

"Good night, Jemma."

Once she left the kitchen, he blew out a breath and tried not to think about what a huge mistake he was making by staying here in the B&B with Jemma and Trey.

He wasn't supposed to get personally involved, remember? Why on earth had he agreed to sleep here, and worse, in her favorite room?

Of all the idiotic ideas, this had to be the biggest one yet. He was going out on a limb here, putting his job in jeopardy, in order to protect Jemma and Trey.

He added more ice to the makeshift cold pack and wrapped it in a plastic bag so it wouldn't get the sheets wet. Then he made his way up the massive curved staircase to the second-floor bedrooms. The yellow room wasn't difficult to find, and he could swear he smelled daffodils as he washed up in the bathroom. The room was cute and homey, breezy yellow curtains covering the windows and several beautiful scenic oil paintings decorating the walls. It was nicer than his apartment by a mile. He gratefully crawled into bed. Placing the ice pack between his temple and the pillow and despite the incessant headache, he fell asleep.

At various points throughout the night, he dreamed Jemma was there, hovering over him asking him questions. Each time he reached out for her, his fingers found nothing but air.

The jarring sound of a ringing phone dragged him awake. Bright sunlight poured in through the windows, illuminating the yellow walls. It took a minute to remember he was in Jemma's favorite room of the B&B. His headache wasn't gone but seemed more tolerable as he groped for his phone.

"It's right here." Jemma's voice from the doorway startled him. "I'm sorry to wake you, but some guy is demanding to speak with you."

"What time is it?" he asked, scrubbing his palm over his bristly chin.

"Eight o'clock," she admitted, her expression full of guilt. "I know I should have woken you up earlier, but I think it's best for you to take the day off. I've been reading up on head injuries, they can be very serious, and it can take weeks to recover from them."

"I don't have weeks," he muttered, holding out a hand for the phone. He didn't want to admit how much he liked the idea of staying home at least for a day or two. "This is Lewis," he said, answering the phone.

"Hey, Garth, it's Derek. The drunk you brought is ready to be sprung, but I heard we're supposed to wait until you come in to talk to him. And um, you're late for your shift."

"Yeah, sorry about that." He swung his legs over so that he was sitting up on the side of the bed. "Can you stall him for a bit? I'll be there in thirty minutes."

"I will, but he's making noises about getting a lawyer, so you'd better hurry."

"I will, thanks. See you soon." He disconnected from the phone, realizing he was almost out of battery.

It would have been smarter to go straight home, now he was even further behind.

"I've made toast and eggs for breakfast," Jemma said. "I think you should eat before you leave."

"No time," he said, forcing himself to stand. His right shoulder was a bit sore, but he ignored that, too. "I have to get home to change, then report to headquarters."

"I'll create a breakfast sandwich you can eat on the road." She disappeared, leaving him alone.

He used the bathroom, noticing the fresh toothbrush and toothpaste sitting on the edge of the sink. He gladly used them both, wishing there was a razor as well, then headed down to the main level.

"Hi, Policeman," Trey said from his booster seat. The boy swung his legs back and forth, kicking beneath the table. "How come you're not wearin' your badge?"

"I left it at home, but I am going to get it now." He smiled at the boy and then turned to Jemma. "Sorry to leave so quickly like this."

"It's fine, thanks again for staying. I made you breakfast to go." Jemma shoved a napkin-wrapped breakfast sandwich into his hand. He glanced down at the makeshift meal: fried egg, cheese, and a slice of ham on an English muffin. "Check back with me later, okay?"

"I will," he rashly promised. "Bye, Trey, see you later."

Walking down the driveway, he scanned the area for any sign of Cunningham. There was nothing, other than his truck sitting right where he'd left it, apparently unharmed.

Jemma's sandwich tasted amazing, and he quickly ate as he drove back home. His stomach didn't rebel, which he considered a good sign. Twenty minutes later, mostly because he'd decided against shaving, he walked into the sheriff's department headquarters.

"You!" Ahern's eyes were still bloodshot as he glared at Garth. "I demand to be released right now!"

"Okay." Garth approached the cell door but didn't unlock it. "But we need to talk before you leave."

Ahern's gaze darted around the interior of the department as his lip curled. "About what?"

"Jemma McNally."

Ahern flinched in response to the name and took a step back, his eyes dropping to stare at the floor. "What about her?"

"Come on, Ahern, be straight with me. You came here to talk to her, didn't you?"

Ahern shook his head, but didn't meet his gaze. "No, I didn't know she was here."

"You didn't know Jemma McNally lived in McNally Bay?" Garth's tone reflected his disbelief. "You need a better answer than that if you want to get out of here."

There was a long pause, then Ahern sighed. "Okay, yeah. Maybe I considered talking to her. But she lives in that huge house that has guests staying there, so I chickened out."

"Did you drop a baseball card?"

"Nope." The guy avoided his gaze in a way that roused his suspicions. He wasn't a very good liar.

"You're sure?" Garth wished he'd gotten fingerprints from the card.

Ahern's tone turned whiny. "Lemme go. I didn't do nothing wrong."

"Randal Cunningham paid you to come here, didn't he?"

"Huh?" Ahern's confusion looked real. "Who's that?"

Garth stared at Ahern, his thoughts whirling in tandem to his throbbing headache.

Was it really possible this was just a coincidence? That Ahern hadn't been sent by Cunningham after all?

If that was the case, who was Cunningham working with? And how on earth would Garth find his mystery accomplice?

5

A t the last minute, Jemma decided against telling Jazz and Dalton about the events from the previous night. The last thing they needed was to start worrying about her, more than they already were. Besides, she suspected that Garth's attack had been Randal's knee-jerk reaction to finding someone outside. Maybe now that he knew the cops were nearby he'd move on.

She wished Randal would just leave her alone. Her ex didn't really want to share custody of Trey. While they were married, Randal had avoided helping out with feeding and changing their son. It was all women's work.

Jazz and Dalton discussed the ongoing renovation project as they ate. Jemma didn't say much, thinking about Garth's head injury as she cleaned Trey's face and hands before sending him off to play.

She had set her alarm every two hours during the night to go up and check on him, worried that he'd end up going into some sort of coma. He'd always answered her questions accurately, but she could tell by the way he looked at her in confusion that he wasn't himself.

Why had he decided to go into work? Would it be so bad to take a day or two off so that he could fully recover?

Men were stubborn pigheaded creatures, she decided as she scrubbed the counter. Never listening to basic common sense.

"Jemma?"

She belatedly glanced toward Jazz. "Sorry, what?"

Her twin frowned. "Is something wrong? You seem preoccupied this morning. I asked about your plans for the day."

"I'm fine." She pasted a smile on her face. "I was thinking about our grand opening in three days. I need to get up into the attic to go through a few things. I really want to find Grandma's silver candlesticks for the mantle above the fireplace and then finalize the breakfast menu for both Saturday and Sunday."

"Your meals are great, nothing for you to worry about. Especially since our guests come for the view and the quaint atmosphere of the town as much as the meals. And I've been working on some new marketing strategies."

"I know." She appreciated Jazz's attempt to make her feel better. "I was thinking we could play up our Irish heritage by offering a full Irish breakfast."

Jazz's eyes brightened. "That's a great idea!"

"I thought I'd offer something else too, something special each weekend, but wanted the main staple to be the full Irish." Jemma grinned wryly. "Do you think that will go over with our guests?"

"Absolutely. The full Irish along with a breakfast special sounds perfect," Jazz said, nodding enthusiastically. "I love all your recipes."

"Grandma's recipes," Jemma corrected with a wry smile. "She was the genius in the kitchen. I'm a mere apprentice."

"Yeah, right," Dalton chimed in. "I have to agree with Jazz on this one. You can cook for me any day, any time."

Her smile widened, secretly pleased how well her soon-to-be brother-in-law fit into their family. "Have you two decided on a wedding date yet?"

Jazz and Dalton exchanged a long look. "Not yet, I'd really like to have Jonas attend, and so far, he hasn't given us a specific date that he'll be returning stateside, other than to say, soon." Jazz shrugged. "I guess that's the Army for you."

"Yeah, I understand." Jemma missed her brother, too. They all did. She and Jazz had four older brothers: Jesse, Jeremy, Jake, and Jonas. Jonas had been stationed in Afghanistan for twelve months already, not even allowed to return for either of their grandparent's funerals. And while they could video-chat and email, it wasn't the same. "Hopefully, he'll be able to give us details in the next week or so."

"I hope so." Jazz's expression was troubled for a moment, then cleared. "At least Jake agreed to come from Ireland, which is good news." Her twin's expression clouded. "I only wish our parents were still alive."

Jemma went over to give Jazz a quick hug. "I know, I wish the same thing."

Jazz returned her embrace, then subtly wiped her eyes and cleared her throat. "Hey, I have an idea. Why don't you take a little time for yourself? Dalton and I will finish cleaning up here while keeping an eye on Trey."

Her sister's offer was sweet and tempting. She loved Trey more than anything on this earth, but being a single parent wasn't easy. "Thanks, Jazz."

"Go on." Jazz made a shooing motion with her hand. "Leave the rest to us."

Jemma draped the dishcloth over the faucet and wiped her hands on a towel. "I'll be quick," she promised.

"Take your time," Jazz insisted.

Jemma found herself relaxing in the hot shower, reveling in having a few minutes of peace and quiet. She lingered longer than she should have, then took more time to rub lotion over her skin.

When she realized she was doing all this to look and smell nice for Garth, she inwardly winced. Reminding herself she didn't need additional complications in her life, she pulled on her oldest, most comfy pair of jeans and an old threadbare Chicago Blaze rugby shirt.

Her first serious boyfriend, Clay Ryan, had played rugby. Personally, she'd thought the sport was ridiculously dangerous, but that didn't stop her from rooting for Clay from the sidelines.

Idly, she wondered where Clay was now. They'd gone their separate ways after a year-long relationship. If things had worked out for them, she never would have ended up with Randal.

Then again, that would also mean not having Trey. And giving birth to her son was something she'd never regret.

But still, the rugby shirt reminded her of happier times, which is why she'd hung onto it for all these years.

Jemma returned to the kitchen in a better mood, stopping abruptly when she saw Garth seated at the kitchen table, holding Trey in his lap.

"Jemma, we were just hearing about the events from last night," Jazz said in a brittle tone that betrayed her disappointment. "Why didn't you tell us?"

"I should have," Jemma admitted, wondering why she'd bothered to avoid the subject in the first place. She should have known the truth would come out eventually. "I didn't want you to worry. I'm sure Garth being here last night took Randal by surprise and scared him off."

Garth sent her an apologetic look but shook his head. "I don't think we should assume anything at this point. It may not have been Cunningham who assaulted me, but someone he hired. I don't think it's Ahern, though. He was locked up in jail overnight and didn't recognize Cunningham's name."

"Who's Ahern?" Jazz asked.

Jemma had almost forgotten about Stephan Ahern showing up in McNally Bay. "He's the father of one of my students. I reported him to Child Protective Services for abuse." She turned toward Garth, disconcerted to see how natural he looked holding her son. "Surely you don't believe Ahern showed up here by accident?"

"No, Ahern admitted he came on purpose. Apparently just seeing your new sign at the entrance of the driveway identifying this as McNallys' B and B scared him off. He assumed you had guests staying here already."

"Is there anything else going on that I should know?" Jazz demanded, obviously upset.

"That's all of it," Jemma assured her. The sense of peace and serenity evaporated, leaving a feeling of dull resignation behind. She absolutely needed to get back to yoga. Hadn't she seen a sign offering yoga classes at the local gym the last time she'd gone to the grocery store? She made a mental note to see if they offered childcare services, too. "Thanks for letting me know about Ahern."

"I told him to get out of Clark County or face additional charges," Garth said. "I waited and watched while he packed up his tent and drove away. I don't think you need to worry about him any longer."

"That's something, I guess." She knew she owed it to Jazz and Trey to remain positive. "Well, thanks again for letting me know the outcome."

Garth didn't appear inclined to leave. Trey got antsy and wiggled off the deputy's lap and ran back to his mini car collection spread out between the tables she'd placed in the living room turned dining room. She believed their guests would appreciate having breakfast with a stunning view of the lake.

"Jemma, could we talk for a minute, alone?" Garth shifted in his seat as if he were embarrassed.

"Dalton and I were just leaving," Jazz quickly interjected. "We have a lot of work to do."

"We were?" Dalton asked. Jazz scowled at him, and he looked abashed and nodded. "Oh, yeah. We were. Jemma, we'll check in on you later."

"I'm fine, no need to keep popping over," she said sternly.

"You don't want to feed us?" Dalton asked with a forlorn look on his face.

She rolled her eyes and smiled, unable to hold a grudge against her twin's fiancé. "Yes, I'll feed you."

"Thanks, sis." Dalton came over and gave her a quick hug. Jazz hugged her, too.

"Next time, confide in me, please?" her twin whispered.

"I will." Jemma watched as Dalton ushered Jazz out through the great room toward the front door. Vowing to make up with her sister later, Jemma lifted the teapot, adding hot water to her lukewarm tea, then came over to sit across from Garth. "What is it? Did you learn something more about Randal?"

"Yeah, I checked in with his lieutenant again, who claimed that Cunningham reported to work at seven thirty this morning. I know there was plenty of time to attack me at twelve-thirty and drive back to Bloomington, but Young is making noises about filing a harassment complaint against us, so I dropped the issue for now."

"Randal is slick enough to pull it off."

"Yeah, maybe. But I don't think Cunningham is doing his own dirty work, which is why his lieutenant is so angry with me. Think about it, why would Cunningham take the risk of being up all night and reporting to duty in the morning as assigned? It seems like asking for trouble."

There wasn't a good answer for that.

"Listen, I think we need to consider the fact that he's hired someone else to do all this. After all, the guy who came to pick up Trey from school didn't fit Cunningham's description, right?"

"Right." She nodded, trying to ignore the sinking feeling in her gut.

"Jemma, I want to do a criminal background check on your guests who are coming to stay this weekend."

Her gaze shot to his. "You really think he'd hire someone to stay here as a guest?"

"I believe anything is possible," Garth said somberly. "And I'd rather be safe than sorry."

She took a sip of her tea, then set it aside and reached for the laptop computer. She logged in and pulled up the guest list. There were four couples registered to stay in the B&B this weekend, three married couples and one engaged couple. She and Jazz had hoped to convince the engaged couple to consider booking one of their gazebo wedding packages. They'd even given them the blue room, the one they'd designed as the honeymoon suite, hoping to encourage a return visit sometime soon.

Dutifully writing down their names, she handed the list to Garth. "I highly doubt any married or engaged couples registered to stay here are involved in something criminal."

"I know, but I still need to check them out." Garth folded the paper and tucked it in his pocket. "I, um, was wondering if you'd mind if I stayed here in the yellow room again tonight."

She blinked and gaped. "You want to stay here?"

"Yeah. If it's not too much trouble." He shrugged. "I'd rather be close by, in case there's another attempt to break in or worse."

"Oh, sure. Of course." Jemma told her traitorous heart to settle down. This wasn't Garth wanting to get close to her personally.

He only wanted to keep her safe.

And that's what she wanted, too. Right?

Right.

Although telling herself that was far easier than actually believing it.

GARTH ROSE TO HIS FEET, knowing he needed to get back to work. "I'll see you later this evening, okay? I'll stop by after dinner."

"You can join us if you'd like," she offered. "I have to cook for everyone else, adding one more isn't a problem."

He hesitated, knowing he should decline, but the thought of making something himself, or returning to Daisy's Diner, wasn't very appealing.

"What if I brought dinner instead? Do you like Chinese? Chen Lee's has great takeout."

Her eyes lit up. "That would be great. But don't forget to bring enough for Jazz and Dalton, too."

"I won't. Will Trey eat Chinese?"

"I'm not sure he's tried it, but generally he's not a picky eater."

"I'll make sure to get some honey chicken for him." Glad to be contributing, he smiled. "See you around six?"

"Sounds good." She followed him to the door. "Thanks again, Garth. For everything."

He turned to look down at her deep brown eyes, fighting the need to kiss her. "Thank you for keeping an eye on me last night."

The corner of her mouth tipped up in a smile. "I wasn't sure you remembered."

"I do, although at the time I thought I was dreaming." The air between them shimmered with awareness, and he had to curl his fingers into fists to prevent himself from reaching for her and cuddling her close.

For a long moment, neither of them moved. He wanted to believe he saw the same attraction he felt shimmering in her chocolate gaze.

"Mommy! Come play wif me!" Trey's voice was like a bucket of cold water splashing in his face.

"Coming," Jemma called, taking a small step back. Her smile seemed sad. "See you later, Garth."

"Six," he repeated, then forced himself to turn away. He could feel the heat of her gaze on his back as he strode to his squad car.

But when he looked back at the doorway, Jemma was gone.

Inwardly grimacing at his foolish imagination, he made a Y-turn in the wide driveway and then headed out onto the highway. His head still hurt, but ignoring the pain was becoming second nature. He returned to the Pine Cone Campsite to make sure Ahern hadn't doubled back and, after confirming the guy's

vehicle was nowhere to be found, went on to scope the place out for a sign of anyone who looked as if they fit the description of the guy who'd tried to pick up Trey from preschool.

No luck.

At lunchtime, he picked up a fish sandwich to go and returned to his desk at headquarters. While he ate, he ran background checks on the four couples who had registered to stay at The McNallys' B&B.

They all came out clean, aside of a few speeding tickets and one five-year-old DUI. He proceeded to run credit checks as well but found no obvious signs of financial difficulties either. In fact, all four couples appeared, at least on paper, to be nice people looking for a weekend away.

He downed a couple of ibuprofen for his headache and stared at the names Jemma had given him. Maybe he was being paranoid. It wouldn't be smart for Cunningham to hire someone to boldly register as a guest to get inside the B&B.

Sitting back in his chair, he gently probed the swelling on his right temple. The skin was beginning to turn dark purple, but he sensed he was lucky the injury hadn't been worse.

Assaulting a cop was a stupid, reckless move. He wanted to believe the jerk would continue to make mistakes.

Since the radio was quiet, Garth spent another thirty minutes trying to identify Cunningham's friends. He knew the guy hung out with other cops, but maybe there was someone else he was friends with, not associated with law enforcement.

But his search was futile. He'd need to find out from Jemma if there was anyone in particular from Cunningham's past who may be swayed into doing something as despicable as attempting to kidnap a kid, stalking a cop's ex-wife, and assaulting a cop.

Seemed incredible that anyone would need money that badly to do something so drastic.

Dejected, he stood and walked back out to his squad car. It was close to three in the afternoon, time to make another loop through town. He knew that just having law enforcement visible was enough to deter many a criminal act.

Thankfully, Clark County wasn't a hot bed of illegal activity. Oh, they had the usual drug abuse issues that everyone else across the country struggled with and the accompanying petty theft. But the closest thing to attempted murder he'd seen recently was when Jazzlyn's ex-fiancé had tried to cut her throat.

And now another McNally sibling was in trouble. Maybe he should be glad the McNally brothers hadn't shown up yet. He'd learned from Jazz last month there were a total of four McNally brothers, all older than the twins. If the brothers attracted as much trouble as the twins had, they'd need more police support. There were only a couple of deputies on duty at a time.

Thinking of Jazzlyn's case made him remember old Leon Tate and the animosity he held toward the McNallys. Maybe he should visit the Tates, see if he could convince them to come clean about whatever is bothering them.

With a destination in mind, he drove through town and turned right on Maple Street. Leon Tate didn't live far from Betty Cromwell, and he liked to cruise past her Cape Cod on a regular basis too. Elderly residents were often viewed as easy targets by drug users, and as much as Betty drove him crazy with her nonstop gossip, he didn't want to see anything bad happen to her.

He pulled into Leon Tate's driveway when a call came

through his radio. "Unit ten, there's a vandalism call outside the Friendly Fitness Center."

"Unit ten, responding." He threw the gearshift into reverse and backed out of Leon Tate's driveway. He hit the strobe lights and maneuvered through traffic to the Friendly Fitness Center, located on the opposite side of Main Street, a few blocks down from the grocery store.

When he turned in, he was shocked to see Jemma standing in the doorway, holding Trey on her hip. Her face was pale, and there were damp tear tracks on her cheeks.

He leaped from the car and rushed to her side, pulling her and Trey into his arms. "Jemma! Are you all right?"

"Yes." Her voice was low and husky, muffled against his chest. Embracing her felt right, and he didn't want to let her go. "But the van isn't."

The van? Without releasing his hold, he glanced over his shoulder. It wasn't difficult to find the older model green Dodge van in a parking stall several spaces down from the front door of the fitness center. A red haze of fury clouded his vision when he realized that all four tires had been slashed with a knife.

Cunningham or his puppet had struck again.

6

Jemma couldn't help leaning on Garth, her knees weak and shaky. His woodsy scent and the reassuring comfort of his arms around her waist were exactly what she needed.

This was what she thought she'd have with Randal.

Strength. Support. Caring.

Instead what he'd given her was fear, intimidation, and cruelty. She blinked back a fresh wave of tears, hit by an overwhelming wave of despair. Would this ongoing torture never stop?

Garth's arms tightened around her. "Did you just notice this when you came out of the gym?"

She nodded, her throat tight with tears, making it impossible to speak. The peaceful Zen feeling she'd managed to find after forty-five minutes of yoga had vanished in an instant.

The slashed tires had brought her back to cold, hard reality.

"Okay, I need to do some interviews, see if one of the pedestrians happened to see anyone lurking around."

She closed her eyes for a second, wishing she could stay with him like this indefinitely.

But of course, she couldn't. Garth had a job to do, and she had a son to care for and protect. Jemma dragged in a deep breath and found the courage to lift her head and take a step backward. Since her knees still felt weak, she leaned back against the doorframe and subtly shifted Trey in her arms.

Garth didn't leave right away but placed his index finger under her chin, lifting her face so he could look at her. "I'm going to take care of this, Jemma. Once I finish interviewing the staff, I'll drive you and Trey home."

His gentle tone was nearly her undoing. She blinked away renewed tears and took a moment to clear her throat, finally finding her voice. "Thank you."

He cupped her cheek with his hand and swiped the dampness away from her cheeks with the soft pad of his thumb. The gesture was surprisingly intimate, and it was all she could do not to throw herself back into his arms.

Garth moved away, and she turned her attention to her son. The way he was sucking his thumb, a habit she'd thought they'd broken, it was obvious Trey had picked up on her emotional distress.

"Guess what?" She forced a cheerful note in her tone. "We're going to get to ride in the police car. Won't that be fun?"

Trey blinked, then removed his thumb from his mouth. "Will we hear the sirens?"

"No, the police only use sirens when there's an emergency."

Trey frowned and pointed at Garth's squad car. "But the lights are on, does that mean there's a 'mergency?"

"No. Everything is fine." She hated the thought of her

son being exposed to danger like this. The four slashed tires had been a terrifying message, proof that either Randal himself or someone else was following her.

How else would her ex have known about her trip to the fitness center? She'd only decided to attend shortly after lunch and hadn't told anyone.

Not even Jazz and Dalton.

She shivered and scanned the faces of the gaping onlookers that had gathered around when Garth had driven up in the Clark County Sheriff's Department vehicle. She didn't see anyone who looked guilty, although she noticed there was an old guy leaning on a cane who wore a smirk on his face.

As if on cue, Garth approached the guy. She was too far away to hear their conversation, but the old man's smirk vanished, replaced by a deep scowl. After a few minutes of what appeared to be terse conversation, the old guy turned and slowly stumped away.

Trey grew antsy, so she gently set him on his feet, but held firmly onto his hand. "Stay by Mommy," she warned.

He tugged on her hand. "Wanna see the police car."

She relented, allowing Trey to lead her toward Garth's vehicle. Then she picked him up, so he could see the spinning red and blue lights up close. He reached out a hand to touch them, giggling with excitement. "Pretty. Like Christmas."

Not exactly, she thought with a small sigh.

Trey stared, entranced by the twirling lights. When he grew heavy, she set him down. He rubbed his hand over the lettering etched on the side. "Police," he said, as if pretending to read.

"Clark County Sheriff's Department," she said, pointing

at each word as she spoke. "Deputy Lewis works for the Sheriff's Department."

Trey looked confused. "Police? I have a police badge, right?"

"Yes, police," she agreed, suddenly weary. There was no easy way to describe the difference between a sheriff's deputy and a regular police officer to a three-year-old.

Fifteen minutes later, Garth walked over. "Ready to get home?"

"Very. I'll just grab Trey's car seat from the van." She dug in her purse for the keys, and Garth gently took them from her.

"Stay here with Trey. I'll get it."

There was a small part of her that wanted to insist she could do these things on her own, but she told herself to let it go. Garth wasn't trying to be controlling, the way Randal had been. He was being sweet and kind. Comforting her when she needed it.

Trusting another man, especially a cop, wasn't easy, but somehow Garth had found the perfect balance of being protective and complimentary of her cooking skills. She appreciated having him to lean on in a stressful time like this.

The weight of the van sat heavily on the rims, and she idly wondered if she'd need to replace them as well as the tires. Plus, the stupid thing would have to be towed to a garage. How much would all of that cost? Sure, she had insurance but carried a thousand-dollar deductible.

The van wasn't worth much more than that, but it was all she had. And all she could afford until money started coming in from their business. Randal paid child support, but only the bare minimum since she'd traded that for sole custody.

Garth strapped the car seat in the back of the squad car, then stepped back so she could place Trey inside. The wire cage separating the front seat from the back was intimidating, but her son didn't seem to mind.

"Who was that old guy you were talking to?" she asked, when Garth pulled out of the parking lot.

He glanced at her. "Leon Tate."

The name registered with a click. "Oh yeah, Jazz mentioned something about him holding a grudge against our family. No wonder he was smirking."

"He claims he had nothing to do with slashing your tires, but I haven't taken him off the suspect list just yet."

That surprised her. "Why not? I'm sure this was Randal's handiwork."

Garth nodded. "Your ex is my primary suspect, but I won't rule out anyone without proof." He grimaced. "Unfortunately, no one claims to have seen anyone hanging around your van or the parking lot in general."

"That figures." In her mind, that only pushed Randal higher on the list. Her ex would be too smart to slash tires while someone was looking.

"I'm in jail," Trey announced from the back seat. "It's a 'mergency. You gotta use the sirens."

Garth grinned. "Okay, but only for a minute because driving you home, or even to jail, is not an emergency."

"Sirens," Trey demanded, kicking his feet against the child safety seat. "I wanna hear the sirens."

Garth moved his hand toward the switch, but she quickly stopped him. "Wait, you shouldn't give in," she admonished. "He needs to learn he can't have everything he wants."

Garth hesitated, then shrugged. "Seems like a small thing to give him, after everything he's been through today."

Their gazes clung for a fraction of a second. She smiled and nodded. Garth waited until he was in the driveway of the B&B before he flicked the switch so that the sirens wailed.

Trey clapped his hands over his ears. "Too loud!"

"Okay, it's off now." Garth grinned at her. "Guess he won't be asking for sirens again any time, soon."

"Right?" She couldn't help but smile. After pushing open her passenger-side door, she opened the back door to rescue Trey. He wasn't crying, but he still had his hands over his ears.

"It's okay, Trey." She tugged his hands away from his ears. "See? No more loud noises."

"Bad sirens hurt my ears," Trey said in a solemn tone.

She shook her head and lifted him out of the squad car. When he was on his feet, she set about removing the car seat.

"How do you feel about driving a truck?" Garth asked, taking the car seat from her hands.

She shrugged and kept an eye on Trey. "Not that much different from a van, size-wise. I'm sure Jazz will let me borrow hers."

"I'll loan you mine. The sheriff won't mind if I use the squad car for a while." Garth carried the car seat toward the garage.

"That's nice, but not necessary." She grabbed Trey's hand, unwilling to let him wander too far away, then punched in the code. The door slowly lifted upward. He set the seat inside and then waited for her to close it again.

"I insist." He glanced at his watch. "Listen, I need to finish up my report on your tires, then I'll stop by my place to pick up my truck. I won't forget to grab our Chinese for dinner either. Should be back in an hour."

"Okay. Thanks again for the ride." She decided to wait until later to argue with him about borrowing his truck. "Come on, Trey. Would you like a snack? Maybe animal crackers?"

Her son nodded, his fear over the loud sirens apparently forgotten.

She held the door for Trey, then followed him inside. She stood at the door, watching as Garth drove away.

Feeling vulnerable and alone, she closed and locked the front door, trying to shake off the ridiculous feeling. She'd been constantly looking over her shoulder for Randal since she'd garnered the courage to leave him. She didn't want to regress to that panicky state now.

Jazz and Dalton were right next door.

And Garth would return in an hour. She felt cold despite the warm weather, then reminded herself that whoever might be following her must have noticed how she'd been given a ride home by a sheriff's deputy. She doubted he'd be so quick to make another move against her.

She just wished she knew what would scare the guy off, for good.

GARTH FINISHED his report in record time, then also made arrangements for Jemma's van to be towed to a local garage. He couldn't explain why he'd felt so nervous leaving Jemma and Trey at the B&B alone.

At his place, he tossed his shaving kit and a spare change of casual clothes into his duffel bag. No need for a uniform because he'd switched shifts, picking up Friday so he could be off tomorrow, Wednesday.

He intended to be close at hand the next time her ex-husband, or his vandal-for-hire, struck out at her. At the rate he was going, it wouldn't be long before he made his next move.

The scent of Chinese food filled the interior of his truck as he drove to the B&B. As he pulled into the driveway, he was struck by the odd feeling of coming home.

Crazy, because the B&B was hardly a home. It was a place of business. He was only staying there temporarily. Yet he couldn't deny the yellow room called to him in a way his apartment never could.

Whoa. What was he thinking? This couldn't ever be his home. He sat for a moment, reminding himself that he shouldn't get personally involved with Jemma and Trey. He needed some professional distance in order to protect them.

Glancing at the duffel on the floor of the passenger seat, he realized it was too late.

He'd already crossed the line.

The image of Kate Bruno's face and that of her innocent daughter, Sophie, flashed in his mind, and his heart squeezed with dread. They'd both almost died on his watch.

Because he'd gotten too close. Had let his feelings interfere with his duty. Had thought everything was fine, when it clearly wasn't.

He couldn't, wouldn't do that again. He considered backing out of his request to stay overnight in the B&B, then decided he couldn't disappoint Jemma.

Or risk leaving her and Trey alone and vulnerable.

With an inward sigh, he slid out from behind the wheel, then went around to sling his duffel bag over his shoulder, then pulled out the large white bag of Chinese food.

Jazz answered the front door. "Right on time," she said lightly, although her gaze remained serious. "Jem told us about her van, and I hear you took care of getting it towed, for which we are very grateful. Do you have any leads on who is behind all this?"

He was relieved Jemma had mentioned the news herself. He'd felt bad ratting her out earlier. "Not yet."

"It's her ex-husband," Jazz said firmly.

"Probably," he agreed. "But I can't prove it. And his boss has provided an alibi."

Jazz frowned. "That means he hired someone to do it."

"That's my best guess." He remembered his intent to grill Jemma on who her ex was friendly with, outside of other cops on the Bloomington police force. "Again, not much I can do without some kind of evidence."

"Something smells good," Dalton said as he came into the great room.

"Chinese." Garth handed the bag to Dalton. "I hope there's enough," he joked. "I forgot I was feeding a small army."

Dalton peered into the bag with a frown. "I don't know, I mean this is good for me, but I don't know what the rest of you are going to eat."

For a moment Garth froze, wondering if he was serious. Had he underestimated how much food they'd need?

"Stop it," Jazz chided with a smile. "Garth isn't used to your warped sense of humor. I'm sure there's plenty for all of us."

Feeling foolish and awkward, Garth followed Jazz and Dalton into the kitchen, his gaze zeroing in on Jemma. She wore a pair of slim ankle-length tan slacks with a bright orange blouse that accented the blond highlights in her hair. She looked lovely, and his pulse jumped erratically.

Yep, he'd crossed the line, big time.

"How come you're not wearing your uniform?" Trey asked.

"I'm off duty." He knelt down to look the boy in the eye. "Why don't you call me Garth instead of policeman?"

"Garf?" Trey cocked his head to the side. "Your name is Garf?"

"Rhymes with barf," Dalton teased.

"Deputy Lewis," Jemma said forcefully, crossing over to pick up her son. "You may call him Deputy Lewis. Not barf-er-Garth."

Jazz snickered, and Dalton was grinning broadly as they opened the white containers of food. The three of them were close, and he felt like the odd man out. He didn't have any siblings and wasn't sure how to take some of their joking around. As the containers were put out and plates were filled, Garth began to fear Dalton was right. What if he hadn't bought enough food for everyone? At least Trey seemed to enjoy the honey chicken, asking for more. As they ate and talked, he relaxed when he realized he'd done okay. Sure, they'd put a serious dent in the meal, but there were still a couple of unopened containers.

Dalton finally sat back with a low groan. "Enough. If I eat any more, I'll bust a gut."

"Told you," Jazz said, poking a finger into his flat belly with a wide grin. "Better watch out or you'll get soft."

"Never," Dalton vowed, giving her a quick kiss. Jazz wrapped her arms around his neck, kissing him back.

Garth had to look away from the obvious love shimmering between them. His gaze clashed with Jemma's, and he found himself momentarily lost in the brown depths, searching for something he didn't dare name.

Kate Bruno, he reminded himself sternly. Remember Kate.

"Mommy? Can I have a cookie?" Trey's plaintive voice broke into his thoughts.

"Only one," Jemma said, opening a container full of warm gooey chocolate chip cookies. No one seemed disappointed to forgo the crisp fortune cookies to have chocolate chip, instead.

Dalton reached for one before Jazz could good-naturedly slap his hand. "Yum."

"I thought you were going to bust a gut?" Jemma asked, her gaze innocent.

"There's always room for dessert, especially your baked goods," Dalton said, taking a big bite.

Garth pushed away from the table and began piling the trash together.

"I'll take care of it," Jemma insisted.

He nodded, then backed away, once again feeling as if he didn't belong here. "I, um, need to make a few calls." He hightailed it out of the kitchen, scooping his duffel from the floor and heading up the wide staircase to the second floor.

He was tempted to pick something other than the yellow room but told himself he was being ridiculous. No reason to make more work for Jemma.

It was too early for bed, but the nagging headache was bad enough that he downed another couple of ibuprofen and stretched out on the mattress. Closing his eyes, he relaxed and reveled in the darkness.

He hadn't intended to fall asleep, but when he opened his eyes, he could see through the window that the sun had gone down. The time was close to nine o'clock at night, which meant he'd slept for a few hours.

Rolling off the bed, he stood, relieved that his headache had nearly vanished. He stretched his arm and shoulder, then padded to the door.

At the top of the stairs, he listened for the sound of

voices, indicating Jazz, Jemma, and Dalton were still in the kitchen, but all was quiet.

Moving silently, he went down to the first level, double-checking that the doors were securely locked. Peering through the windows, he didn't see anything suspicious outside either.

At the French doors, he stared at the lake, remembering the night before and how he'd thought everything was quiet then, too.

But he'd been wrong.

Moving away from the French doors, he stood off to the side of the window that overlooked the east side of the house. The same side where he'd been assaulted.

Without moving he watched, searching for a sign of movement. It may be too early for Cunningham or his hired hand to make a move, but he remained where he was for the next thirty minutes.

Everything outside remained quiet and still, so he made his way into the kitchen. He sat at the table for a moment, wondering how to uncover the identity of Cunningham's accomplice.

The frequency of the attacks against Jemma convinced him that her ex had hired someone who was staying close by. He could make a sweep of the motels in the area, but that wouldn't do much good considering he didn't have a name.

The sound of a door opening had him jumping to his feet. Jemma emerged from the master suite, appearing startled by his presence.

"Oh, uh, hi." She hesitated, then walked through the dining area toward the kitchen. "I thought you were asleep."

"I was for a while." He searched her gaze. "Something wrong?"

She sighed and went to the sink to fill her teapot. He

noticed she tended to make tea when she was stressed. "Nothing new," she said softly. "I just keep wondering when Randal will strike again."

He moved forward, wanting, needing to offer some sort of comfort. "Hey, that's why I'm here, remember? I won't let him hurt you or Trey."

The corner of her mouth tipped up in a reluctant smile. "You have no idea how much I appreciate you staying," she admitted.

After turning on the heat beneath her teakettle, she stood close to him.

Too close. He was lost in the cinnamon and vanilla scents that clung to her skin.

He told himself to step back, to remain professional, but his body didn't listen to his brain. His arms reached for her and drew her close.

She slipped her arms up and around his neck. "Garth," she whispered, and his name had never sounded so good.

He wasn't strong enough to resist the sweet temptation he held in his arms. He lowered his mouth to hers and captured her lips in a soul-shattering kiss.

7

J emma felt herself drowning in Garth's kiss, a wave of longing sweeping through her. It had been so long since she'd kissed a man.

Enjoyed kissing a man.

His muscles were warm and solid beneath her fingertips. He tasted of peppermint and combined with his intoxicating woodsy scent proved to be a powerful aphrodisiac. He was sweet, gentle yet passionate in a way she hadn't experienced in a very long time.

Garth broke off their kiss and took gulping breaths of air. "I, um, that was nice, but, um, I need to get some rest."

She leaned back so she could see his face. "Nice?" she repeated. "Is that your way of saying thanks, but no thanks?"

"Jemma." The way he said her name in his low husky voice sent tingles of awareness rippling across her skin. "I—can't do this. I can't get romantically involved."

"Can't? Or won't?" Her challenging tone surprised her, because she normally didn't push like this. If a guy wasn't interested in her, fine. But Garth's kiss had gone from zero to one-sixty in a heartbeat, and she sensed he was impacted by their embrace the same way she was.

"Same thing." He took a step back, his smile not reaching his eyes. "I didn't ask to stay here at the B and B for this. My only goal here is to keep you and Trey safe."

Her earlier bravado melted away, leaving her feeling foolish and vulnerable. "I know you didn't ask to stay for this, but I thought we shared an emotional connection. My mistake. I really do appreciate your dedication to finding Randal." She turned away, wishing the floor would open up and swallow her. "Oh, and I'll pay you back the amount of the towing fee for my van as soon as possible. Good night."

"Jemma, wait." The urgency in Garth's tone gave her pause, and she glanced at him over her shoulder.

"For what?"

"Could we talk for a minute?" He looked miserable, but she forced herself to stay right where she was.

"There's nothing to talk about." She wanted, needed to get out of there before she made another massive error in judgement. "Truly, I understand where you're coming from, and I'm not upset or anything if that's what you're worried about."

"I'm glad. But I'm looking for information regarding Cunningham's closest friends, or allies, or someone who might be indebted to him. Anyone you think he could lure into doing something like this."

Mortified, she realized that her last comment only made the awkward situation worse. He hadn't wanted to talk about personal stuff but about her ex.

Time to pull herself together.

"I don't know many of them by name," she finally said. "Let me think about it, okay? I'll see if I can come up with a list for you in the morning."

"Yeah, sure." He cleared his throat loudly. "Thanks, Jemma. For everything."

"Good night." She quickly navigated between the tables in the dining room so she could gratefully disappear into the master suite.

After closing the door behind her, Jemma leaned against the solid frame, covered her face in her hands, and inwardly groaned at how badly she'd handled that.

Not only had she initiated an apparently unwanted kiss, but she'd acted as if he should be falling all over himself to date her. Honestly, what in the world had happened to her common sense?

Garth could have any woman he wanted, why would he choose to be saddled with a single mom hiding from an abusive ex-husband? Quite clearly, he wouldn't.

She lifted her head and blew out a silent breath. Okay, then, no more late-night rendezvous with Garth. The explosive kiss they'd shared hadn't impacted him the same way it had gutted her. Fine. Dandy. That was her problem, not his. She should be happy that he was willing to offer his protection, what more did she need?

Nothing. Having him here was more than enough.

Although after the way she'd acted tonight, she wouldn't be surprised if he decided to move on in the morning. To head home, wherever that was.

She tossed and turned for the rest of the night, her brain jumping from Garth, to Randal, to her ex's friends, and then back to Garth.

The sun was bright when she woke up, and she looked around the room in confusion. Usually Trey woke her up, but her son wasn't here.

Instantly she bolted out of bed and rushed to the door,

throwing it open. She raked her gaze over the dining area. "Trey?"

"Here, Mommy." Her son waved at her through the doorway between the dining room and kitchen. He was in his booster seat at the table.

Her panicked heart rate slowed, and she stood for a moment, gaping at the picture Garth made wearing her grandmother's rosebud apron and wielding a spatula. "What are you doing?"

He lifted a brow. "Making breakfast." He flipped the burner on under her teakettle and gestured to the pancakes on the griddle. "I may not be the cook you are, but I can manage simple stuff. These are almost ready if you want to join us."

Abruptly self-conscious, she smoothed a hand over her messy hair and tugged at the hem of the baggy T-shirt she used to sleep in over her boxer shorts. "Um, yes. That would be great. Give me a few minutes."

She ducked inside the bedroom and quickly brushed her teeth, pulled her hair back into a ponytail, and changed her clothes. Emerging from the suite a few minutes later, she tried not to be too impressed with the way Garth had taken over the kitchen and had cared for her son.

"Smells delicious," she said, dropping into a seat beside Trey. Her son's face was liberally smeared with maple syrup, but she still pressed a kiss to his temple. "How's breakfast?"

"Yummy in my tummy." Trey took another bite. "I like Barf's flapjacks."

"Garth. I mean, Deputy Lewis," she corrected.

The teakettle whistled. Garth set a package of tea bags and a mug next to her. Feeling pampered, she pulled out a tea bag and placed it in the mug. Garth poured steaming hot water in her cup, then turned back to the stove. "How many flapjacks would you like?"

"Two is fine, although here in the Midwest we call them pancakes."

"Same difference." He slid a plate with two pancakes in front of her. "My foster mother always called them flapjacks, so that's how I think of them. And yeah, okay, you're right. Susan grew up in Louisiana."

"Told you," she said with a laugh. Then her smile faded as she realized that Garth had grown up in foster care. Losing her parents and grandparents had been bad enough, but not having her siblings was incomprehensible. She couldn't imagine not having any family and wondered if Garth knew anything about his.

"What's the matter? Are you afraid to try them?"

"Of course not." Using the edge of her fork, she cut into her pancakes and took a bite. "Hmm. These are incredible. Your foster mother taught you well."

"Yes, she did." There was an underlying note of seriousness to his tone. It was on the tip of her tongue to ask more about his past but told herself not to be nosy.

"Can I go fishin'?" Trey asked.

She hid a grimace. Worms, yuck. "Oh, I don't think we have a fishing pole or anything to use as bait. But that's a good idea, Trey. I'll look into getting those things sometime soon."

"I have a fishing pole," Garth offered. "And I'm off work today, so I don't mind taking him fishing."

"Really?" She eyed him curiously over her tea. "You like to fish?"

He shrugged. "Why not? I can't say I'm a professional or anything, but I should be able to keep him out of your hair for a while. If you'd like some time alone to get things done."

She thought about her desire to get into the attic to find the candlesticks. "I would like that, very much. Thank you."

He waved her off. "No need to thank me, it will be fun."

His idea of fun was different from hers, but whatever. She wasn't about to argue.

"Maybe you could write out that list for me while we're down at the lake," he said, digging into his pancakes. "That way I can work on it this afternoon."

She suppressed a sigh and nodded. "It's not a long list," she warned. "I came up with three names."

"That's better than nothing."

Jemma finished her breakfast and poured herself another cup of tea. She took a moment to jot down the three names of Randal's friends and a brief description of how they knew each other; Kevin Rhymes, his current partner on the Bloomington police force, Ben Skubal, his former partner who was recently promoted into a detective role, and Peter Dunn, an old college roommate.

There were likely others, but Randal had kept her at arm's length from his personal life, telling her she needed to stay home with the baby rather than join him in going out on Friday or Saturday nights. She loved Trey, so taking care of him was no hardship, but she'd resented the way Randal had treated her as the little woman who needed to stay at home.

Especially when he'd come home drunk and mean more often than not. Until things had escalated that fateful night.

Thank goodness for Jazz dropping everything to come to pick up her and Trey. She hadn't maintained any friendships, but family was forever.

Something Garth may not completely understand.

Placing the list in front of Garth, she turned her attention to cleaning up.

"I'll do the dishes," Garth protested. "I've been told I'm a messy cook."

"I'm grateful you bothered to cook at all," she told him honestly. "I can't tell you the last time a man did that for me."

He stared at her for so long, she felt herself blush. She turned to fill the sink with sudsy water. Friends, remember? Nothing more.

Kitchen cleanup duty didn't take long, and Garth asked if she minded if he took Trey along with him to pick up his fishing pole and bait. Letting her son out of her sight wasn't easy, but she told herself that wrapping Trey in a blanket of fear wouldn't do him any favors.

"Of course, have fun. I'll be up in the attic if you need something."

"Sounds good. Come on, Trey. Let's go for a ride." Garth lifted her son into his arms and strode toward the door. The sight of them together made her breath catch in her throat.

It was good for Trey to have a positive male role model in his life. Someone to look up to.

So why was she longing for more?

Enough. She had no idea how long Trey would be satisfied with his fishing expedition so there was no time to waste. There was a passageway into the attic from the ceiling in the hallway between the green and yellow rooms.

Using a stepladder, she grasped the cord and carefully pulled the foldaway staircase down. A cloud of dust accompanied it. She coughed and waved it away.

There was a light at the top of the stairs, a dim bulb that didn't illuminate the entire area. There were other bulbs strategically placed along the way, and she walked through the boxes and broken furniture to turn them on.

Propping her hand on her hips, she looked around in

dismay. The stuff up here looked to be in worse shape than she remembered. Searching for the silver candlesticks might be a futile effort, but she had to try.

When she and Jazz were kids, they loved playing up here. They'd hang sheets from one nail to another, creating two forts where they could pretend to be living in their own apartments as neighbors.

Unfortunately, their lives had taken different paths, Jazz hadn't found a job to complement her marketing degree, so she'd gone into real estate. Jemma had become a schoolteacher, married Randal, and had given birth to Trey. After that, Randal had insisted she stay home to care for their son, and she remembered Jazz telling her that she needed to stand up for herself.

But at the time, she hadn't listened. Until Jazz had been forced to come to her rescue.

After leaving Randal she'd gone back to teaching second grade. Until the incident with Trey had sent her moving on to McNally Bay.

She and Jazz were still close, more so now that they were living in the same place and kicking off a new business together. But she often wondered what her life would have been like if they hadn't drifted apart after college.

She told herself the past didn't matter, what was important was that she and Jazz were together now. Hopefully, their four older brothers would make good on their promise to come and visit this summer as well.

The B&B was a joint investment, with Jemma and Jazz getting a larger cut for doing the work. Jazz was going to help serve guests and clean rooms, while doing the marketing and the financials. Jemma would do all the cooking, as well as helping out with the other tasks. A true partnership.

Jemma reached for the closest box. Those silver candlesticks had to be in here somewhere.

The first box was filled with old clothes from what looked like her grandmother's early days. Jemma pulled out an old sequined flapper dress, in surprisingly decent shape. There were a few small holes that probably could be fixed.

She frowned, trying to envision what her grandmother had looked like wearing the dress. Maybe there were old photographs somewhere. Then again, maybe the dress hadn't belonged to her grandmother but to someone else. Grandma had died in her mid-eighties, which meant she would have been born in the early thirties, not the roaring twenties.

Gram had a few sisters, though. Old enough to have worn the dress? Maybe. Either way, she couldn't bear to put the dress back in the box, so she carefully set it aside. There had to be something on the internet that would explain the best way to preserve antique clothing.

The next few boxes weren't much help either, no silver candlesticks. Moving deeper into the attic, she found a very old large trunk. Maybe from when her great-grandparents immigrated here from Ireland?

Her fingers itched to see what treasures might be inside, but a large furry spider abruptly dropped down mere inches in front of her face.

"Yeeiiikkk!" Frantic, she jerked away and stumbled backward, to put more distance between her and the hairy beast. The heel of her shoe caught the corner of another box, and she landed hard on top of it, coughing as she was once again enveloped in a cloud of dust.

"Good grief." Her heart was racing, and she put a hand on her chest as if that alone would slow it down. Glancing over toward the trunk, she noticed the spider still hung there from his sticky web, spinning in circles, taunting her. She shivered and rose off the box while keeping far away from the spider, deciding the trunk could wait for another day.

Viewing the box she'd tripped over as a sign, she opened that one next. Intrigued, she saw the old family Bible sitting on top, along with the twin silver candlesticks tucked in opposite corners. The silver was badly tarnished but still recognizable. She set them aside, then pulled out the old Bible, too. Had it belonged to her grandmother? Or her great-grandmother?

She opened the first page to see if there was a family tree inside, but there wasn't one. The words were in English, not Gaelic, so she had to believe it hadn't been brought over from Ireland. Still, she wasn't sure how old it was. With a sense of excitement, she paged through the Bible, wondering if she could get an antique expert to gauge the age of the book.

Beneath the Bible was a folded letter, the paper yellowed with age. Curious, she took it out and carefully unfolded it. The handwriting was thin and a bit shaky, the ink was faded to the point it was difficult to read.

She took the letter closer to the light, far from the spider, and began to read:

Dearest Lucy,

My world is dark without you in it. I don't understand how this happened, and I'm finding it difficult to move on without you.

Life is so precious yet so brief. In one fleeting moment it's gone, as if it had never been. I've searched the Bible for answers but have found no solace to ease my pain. Some would say I haven't tried hard enough, and that may be true. It isn't easy to dissect one's mistakes, holding them up to the glaring light of day.

This suffering is my price to pay.

Always, J.

Jemma frowned, trying to add context to the cryptic note. Lucy was a woman obviously, but who was J? Her grandparents were Joan and Jerry McNally, both *J* names. And they'd continued the tradition by calling her father, Justin. Who in turn added to the madness by naming all six of their children names starting with *J*.

She read the words a second time, feeling certain the words were written by a man. Maybe it was the hint of a forbidden romance and the way it was signed, "Yours, J."

It was also fairly clear that Lucy, whoever she was, had died. *Life is so precious yet so brief . . .*

The note was old, and worthless, but she couldn't seem to set it aside. It had to be written either by her father or her grandfather. Jemma carried the candlesticks down to the kitchen to polish them, then went back to the attic to bring the note and Bible down, too.

As she worked on unveiling the brilliance of the silver beneath the tarnish, she couldn't help going back over that letter.

Who was Lucy? And what relationship did she have with a member of the McNally family?

8

Taking a three-and-a-half-year-old with you to run errands was truly an adventure. Garth had underestimated how quickly they'd be able to get his fishing pole, tackle, and bait. By the time they'd returned to the B&B and settled on the shore, a full hour had passed.

"Me! Me!" Trey jumped up and down beside him. "I wanna fish."

"You will. First, we have to put a worm on the hook." He bent down so Trey could see what he was doing. "The worm is food for the fish. Now, I'm going to help you cast, okay?"

"Okay."

Garth covered Trey's small hands and then jerked the rod, sending the worm and bobber out to the water. It didn't go very far, but the lake was deep so he hoped they'd get lucky.

"Hold the pole steady, like this." He kept his hands on the fishing pole, fearing Trey might let go. "See the bobber in the water? When it goes under the water, that means we may have caught a fish. When that happens, I want you to reel it in."

Trey stared at the yellow and red bobber intently for all of five minutes. Then his gaze began to wander. "I see a boat!"

"That's a speedboat." He remembered what Jemma had said that first day, about how the sailboat had reminded Trey of his father. "Does your daddy have one like that?"

Trey nodded but didn't elaborate. A speedboat was different from a sailboat, but apparently, they all were alike in a child's eyes.

"Have you seen your daddy lately?" He tried to keep his tone casual.

"Yep." Trey nodded again.

His gut clenched. "Where did you see him?"

"At home." Trey wiggled and gasped. "Do we have a fish?"

The bobber had only gone down in the trough of a wave. "Not yet. Where at home? Turn around so you can see the house. Can you point to the place where you saw him?"

"No. At *home*," Trey repeated as if he were dense.

Garth realized the boy meant at his old house, rather than here at the B&B. The McNally mansion must seem too new to the child, not yet considered home. Garth dropped the subject, realizing that attempting to get credible information from a toddler wasn't smart. "Look, Trey! The bobber went down. Reel it in!"

Trey let go of the fishing pole so he could turn the reel. Garth quickly grabbed it before it could fall, then helped to keep the pole steady, while Trey labored over the task. Garth feared the fish had gotten away, but when he lifted the tip out of the water, a tiny carp dangled from the end of the line.

"A fish! A fish!" Trey jumped up and down again, full of excited energy. "I caught one!"

"You sure did." He finished reeling in the carp. He held the end of the line. "Can you hold it like this so I can take a picture?"

"Yeah." Trey took the line, nearly dropped it, then managed to hold it up. Trey grinned as Garth snapped several pictures.

"Good job. This fish is pretty small, though, so we need to throw him back."

Trey's lower lip trembled. "I don't wanna throw him back."

Garth knelt beside him. He decided against explaining the DNR rules about fishing. "He's a baby fish, Trey. I think he might be lonely without his mommy and daddy. Wouldn't you be lonely without your parents?"

Trey pursed his lips and nodded. "You're right. We gotta let him loose."

"Good boy." Garth unhooked the baby carp and then let him go in the water. The little guy quickly swam away. "See? I bet he went right to his mommy and daddy."

The boy glanced up at him. "Are you gonna be my new daddy?"

Whoa. Garth rocked back on his heels. Where had that come from? "Um, well, you see . . ." He cleared his throat and tried to think of a way to redirect the kid. "What happens first is that your mommy falls in love. When she and the man she loves get married, that's when you'll get a new daddy."

"I want you to be my new daddy." Trey threw his arms around Garth's legs. "My mom likes to marry policemans."

Probably not anymore, he thought with a grimace. Still, the kid was adorable, so he reached down and hauled him up into his arms. "I like you, too, Trey. We'll be friends, okay?"

Trey nodded, seemingly satisfied with that response. The kid hugged him and then wiggled in his arms, as if eager to be put down.

Garth set him on his feet. "Do you want to fish some more?" he asked. He gestured toward the container filled with night crawlers. "I'll bait the hook for you."

At first Trey nodded eagerly, but then he frowned. "What if we catch another baby fish? I don't want to take him from his mommy."

"We can always let him go," he said gently. When Trey still looked indecisive, he backed off. "Never mind, we'll try fishing another day. Right now, let's take a walk along the lakefront."

"Let's run!" Trey said, taking off as fast as his chubby legs would take him. The kid took a big lead, considering he was less than a third of Garth's size.

He hurried to catch up with the boy, horrified at the thought of him falling in the water, or worse, under his watch. Out of nowhere, a memory of Kate and Sophie laughing at the park crept into his mind.

He ruthlessly shoved it away.

"You can't catch me," Trey said with a giggle. The boy changed directions, heading away from the water, into someone's backyard.

"No, Trey." Garth infused authority in his tone. "We can't go onto other people's property."

The child either didn't hear him or chose not to listen. A dog let out a sharp bark, causing his chest to tighten with terror.

"Trey!" His voice was sharp with fear. "Stop right there!"

This time the boy did as he was told, at the same moment a large yellow furry dog came running from the house, heading straight for Trey.

Garth put on a spurt of speed and scooped the kid up off the ground seconds before the dog arrived. Thankfully, the animal was friendly, sniffing and wagging its tale as it sniffed Garth's shoes.

"Frieda! Get back here right now!" A woman he estimated to be in her mid-fifties came out of the back door. "Don't worry, she's harmless. Except of course for possibly licking you to death."

"I see that." Thank God. Garth's heart still thundered in his chest at the close call. "Sorry, we didn't mean to trespass."

"Not a problem. Frieda, now!" The woman took several steps toward the dog, who whirled and ran back to her. "Frieda had a litter of puppies over a month ago, they'll be ready to go to good homes in another week or so if you and your son are interested. She's a Goldendoodle and doesn't shed."

The hopeful tone in the woman's voice made him smile. He recognized her from being around town but had never responded to any calls to her home, which was probably a good thing. "Trey isn't my son, so it's not my decision. I'll let his mom know, okay?"

"Great. My name is Erica Tang. I have male and female puppies to choose from."

"I'm Garth Lewis, and this is Trey McNally. His mom owns the B and B."

"Oh." Erica's expression fell. "I'm not sure a puppy would be welcome in a B and B."

Garth realized she was right. "Probably not, but it can't hurt to ask."

Erica nodded but didn't look happy when she turned to take Frieda back inside.

Garth turned and carried Trey back to the lakeshore.

Despite the fact that he'd only been with the boy for a couple of hours, he was suddenly exhausted. How did single parents do it? How did Jemma manage, day in and day out? He had no idea.

She deserved a medal. Especially considering she rarely let Trey's rambunctious and sometimes trying behavior get to her.

"Where are we going?" Trey asked.

"Home." He remembered Trey's earlier confusion and added, "To your new home. The big yellow house you now live in with your mom."

"Okay." This time, Trey seemed content to be carried, resting his head on Garth's shoulder. "Will Mommy let me have a puppy?"

Puppy? Oh boy. He was in trouble. Big trouble. He never should have had that conversation in front of Mr. Big-Ears. "I don't know, she's already pretty busy taking care of you. She might not have time for a puppy."

"My mom can do anything," Trey said with confidence.

Yeah, Garth thought. Jemma could do anything, since she was practically Wonder Woman, but he sensed what she was going to do was give him a stern lecture about raising a small child's hopes up about getting a dog.

After that? She'd probably throw him out on his back-side, refusing to speak to him ever again.

JEMMA WAS IN THE BASEMENT, moving a load of laundry from the washer to the dryer when she heard Trey and Garth return.

"When are you gonna ask her about the puppy?" Trey demanded.

Puppy? Her stomach clenched. Oh no. He wouldn't. Garth wouldn't promise Trey something like that.

Would he?

"Trey, I told you before, your mom is already super busy with her new business and taking care of you. She probably doesn't have time for a puppy."

No, she certainly did not. Besides, having a puppy underfoot while managing a B&B was just asking for trouble. Would they need additional insurance to cover dog bites? She shuddered at the thought.

She tossed a fabric softener sheet among the damp clothes and closed the lid and started the dryer. Squaring her shoulders and silently berating Garth for bringing up the subject of a puppy in the first place, she returned upstairs.

"Hi, Trey. How many fish did you catch?" She kept her tone light but gave Garth a dark, steely glare.

He winced, picking up on her not-so-subtle message that she'd heard the conversation. "Only one, right, Trey?"

"Cause he was a baby fish and needed to go back to live with his mommy and daddy." Her son ran over to give her a hug. "Then we saw the doggie, and I was scared at first, but she was real nice. The lady said she has puppies, Mom. Can I have one? Please? Can I?"

"I'm pretty sure the puppies need to stay by their mommy, too. Just like the fish." She narrowed her gaze pointedly at Garth. "Right, Garth?"

"Right." He shifted from one foot to the other, obviously uncomfortable. His gaze was apologetic, but she wasn't ready to let him off the hook yet.

"But the lady said we could have a puppy." Trey could be incredibly single-minded when he wanted something. "We could take the puppy to visit her mommy every day so she wouldn't be lonely."

Did that mean the puppies weren't very far away? Great, just great. "Trey, honey, listen to me. A puppy is a lot of work, and I don't think I can take care of you and a puppy at the same time. Now, are you hungry? Auntie Jazz and Uncle Dalton will be here for lunch soon."

"But I wanna puppy!" Trey's dark brown eyes filled with tears. "Please?"

Dear heaven, what had Garth done to her? How on earth had they stumbled upon a dog and her puppies?

"Trey, that's enough. You heard your mother, she can't take care of you and a puppy." Garth's voice was stern. "How about we play with your cars while she makes your lunch?"

Trey's little shoulders slumped, and he stomped grumpily over to where his mini cars were scattered along the hardwood floor of the dining room.

"I'm sorry," Garth murmured as he walked past to join her son.

"Yeah, me too." It was times like this that made being a single parent incredibly difficult. She understood Trey's desire to have a pet, and she didn't have anything against dogs. Unfortunately, she was allergic to cats, so that narrowed their options.

A goldfish? Hamster? Chinchilla? She wasn't fond of rodent types of pets, but those options were better considering they would have guests staying here.

An image popped into her head of a hamster getting loose and running up the stairs into the guest rooms, and she shuddered.

Nope. That wasn't happening.

She resolutely returned to the kitchen, debating what to make for lunch. If she was only cooking for her and Trey, soup and sandwiches would be more than enough. But Jazz and Dalton were working hard on their renovations and would likely prefer something more.

Deciding on grilled chicken tacos, she went to work. At least they were easy to make. As she diced and grilled the chicken, she reviewed her menu plan for breakfast on Saturday.

After pouring over her grandmother's recipes, she was leaning toward using thick slices of Irish brown bread to make French Toast. She also toyed with the idea of making eggs Benedict, although she wasn't sure how well those would go over. Of course, then she needed to plan out the full Irish breakfast, including blood pudding.

Homemade cranberry muffins and lemon-poppy seed bread would round out the meal. For drinks, she'd offer a variety of fresh juices, coffee, and tea.

When the taco meat was ready, she set about making homemade guacamole. Jazz and Dalton showed up just a few minutes later.

"Hey, Jemma," Dalton greeted her upon entering the room. "Something smells good."

"Tacos," she confirmed.

"Did I hear tacos?" Garth echoed as he joined them. "My stomach is grumbling already."

Men, she thought wryly. "Time to wash up for lunch, Trey."

This time, her son didn't give her any trouble, and she sensed by the wary looks Trey cast her way that her son was trying to prove he was a good boy who deserved a puppy.

And he was, darn it. But puppies and guests didn't mix.

"I see you found Grandma's silver candlesticks," Jazz said, dipping a chip into the guacamole. "They look awesome on the mantle framing the Cliffs of Moher painting from Ireland. I'm jealous that Jake is in Ireland right now."

"Me, too." Then she gave herself a mental head-slap. "Oh, the candlesticks aren't all that I found." Jemma brought the note over to the table and set it in front of her twin. "Check this out."

Jazz read the note, her brow puckered in a frown. "Who's Lucy?"

"No clue. But it's interesting, isn't it? Whoever she was meant something to one of the McNallys."

"Which one?" Dalton asked, leaning over to read the note for himself. "Signing the note J doesn't help much. Your family went nutso with the *J* names."

"I know, right?" Jemma shrugged. "I'm guessing Grandpa or Dad. If we knew how old the paper was, maybe we could narrow it down."

"Very interesting." Jazz's expression turned thoughtful. "I hope it's not some sort of scandalous secret. I'd hate to find out that our father or grandfather was unfaithful."

"Oh, surely not." Jemma stared at the note for a moment, almost wishing she hadn't found it. She idolized the marriages of her parents and grandparents.

"Either way, we have to figure out who Lucy is," Jazz said firmly. "I'm getting the sense that whoever Lucy is, she passed away."

"I'm curious too," Jemma agreed. "It's a mystery."

"Just what we need, another mystery," Garth said wryly.

Jemma couldn't disagree. She took the letter and set it back on the counter, away from the food. "Maybe we should go to the library, see if we can find anything in the old archives about a woman named Lucy connected to the McNallys."

"We could just ask around," Jazz pointed out. Her sister wasn't one for pouring through old books.

"Yeah, I'm sure people like Leon Tate will be happy to fill in our curiosity. The guy smirked as if he were happy to see my slashed tires."

"Betty Cromwell might know something," Dalton piped up. "She's been living here a long time."

"That's not a bad idea," Jemma agreed. "I'll see if I can get in touch with her early next week. After our grand opening."

An abrupt ringing of a phone interrupted the conversation. Garth took the phone from his pocket and stood. "Excuse me, I need to take this call from work."

Jemma nodded, watching as Garth moved into the dining room, out of earshot. "I wonder why they're calling him on his day off?"

"Cops are never off duty," Dalton pointed out.

Jemma couldn't help thinking that Garth wouldn't have been bothered if it wasn't important.

Maybe even something related to Randal. After all, he had promised to get photos of Randal placed into each deputy's squad car. Was it possible someone had seen him? That he was, right now, even in custody? Arrested for violating his no-contact order?

She added a spoonful of guacamole to her chicken taco and took a bite, telling herself not to get her hopes up. Randal was too smart to get caught so easily.

Garth returned moments later, his expression grim. Her gut clenched, and she rose from her seat. "What's wrong? Did something happen?"

"Not exactly." Garth looked indecisive for a moment, then looked her directly in the eye. "Cunningham is waiting to talk to me at headquarters."

"What?" Her knees went rubbery, and she braced herself with her hands on the table. "Here? He's here in McNally Bay? Does this mean you can arrest him?"

"No, unfortunately quite the opposite." Garth carried his plate of half-eaten food to the counter. "He's here to file a formal harassment complaint against me."

"You?" She stared in shock. "Why?"

"I've called to check on him several times, even after his boss told me he was on duty." Garth shook his head. "I'm sure it's nothing more than a bluff, but I have to go. And since I haven't picked up my squad car yet, I'll need to use my truck."

She swallowed hard, grappling with the news. For one thing, she detested the idea of Randal being in town, even this close to her and Trey. Secondly, she didn't trust her ex one bit. There was more to this little fiasco, she was sure of it.

Garth was at the front door when she called out, "Wait!"

He turned and glanced at her. She rushed over. "Garth, please be careful. Randal . . . deep down—there's something wrong with him. I'm afraid he'll try to hurt you."

"Better me, than you."

She sighed. "Don't say that. I don't want anything to happen to you."

The corner of his mouth quirked in a half-smile. "Don't worry. I'm sure this is just a scare tactic on his part. But stay inside, okay?"

"We will." It was a beautiful day out, but she had no intention of exposing her son to the remote possibility of being seen by his father, even from a distance.

She knew from personal experience that any time Randal acted sweet and innocent he was at his most dangerous.

9

Garth didn't like knowing Cunningham was here in McNally Bay. In fact, he wouldn't be surprised if this meeting was nothing more than a front, while someone he'd hired took another shot at getting Trey. What better way to provide an alibi than to be at the Clark County Sheriff's Department while the crime took place?

Yeah, he didn't like this at all. He quickly changed into his uniform, then called Trina on his way to headquarters.

"I need you to keep an eye on the McNally B and B."

"What's going on?"

"Jemma's ex is here, requesting to meet with me. I don't trust the guy. I think he has something planned. Just do your best to stick close, okay?"

"Yeah, sure," Trina agreed. "Let me know how it goes."

"I will," he assured her, although he suspected things wouldn't go well.

Upon entering the building, he noticed Jemma's ex right away. Cunningham rose to his feet, looking exactly like the defensive lineman Jemma had described. Tall with closely cropped dark hair, a dark goatee, and bulky frame as if he lifted weights on a regular basis. A far cry from the skinny, drunk Stephan Ahern. And not even close to the description of the man who'd tried to pick up Trey from his Pre-K program.

"Are you Deputy Lewis?" Cunningham asked with a sneer, looking him up and down as if finding him lacking.

"That's right." Garth did his best to keep his emotions from showing on his face. He didn't offer the guy a seat but remained standing. "And you're Officer Cunningham. What brings you all the way to Clark County?"

"You. I'm putting you on notice that I'm filing a harassment claim against you." Cunningham took a step closer in an attempt to intimidate him. "You need to stop calling my lieutenant, asking about where I am."

Garth didn't retreat. "Actually, I don't. I have a right to investigate a crime, including following up on the whereabouts of a potential suspect. And it's not harassment since I haven't contacted you, personally."

Cunningham's face turned dark red with anger, but the fellow officer managed to keep his tone even. "My lieutenant will be the next one to file a harassment claim."

"That's fine. But again, questions do not constitute harassment. And I'm fairly sure Lieutenant Young understands that."

"Don't mess with me, Lewis." Cunningham's tone turned guttural. "I'm not responsible for any crimes happening here, and you can't prove otherwise."

"Not yet," he agreed. "But it's early in my investigation, so you never know what clues I'll uncover."

"I'll sue you for slander," Cunningham tried, changing tactics. "You're tarnishing my reputation."

"You can try, but remember, it's only slander if it's not true." Garth lifted a brow, refusing to back down. "And since

I haven't finished my investigation, there's still time to uncover the truth."

Cunningham curled his hands into fists and glared at him, as if trying to come up with an additional threat.

"Is that all?" This time, he didn't bother to hide his dismissive tone.

"Watch your step," Cunningham said in a low tone. "The minute you cross the line, I'll be all over you and this entire department."

"It's against the law to threaten a fellow peace officer," Garth pointed out. "But I appreciate you stopping by. It's really great to put a face with a name."

Cunningham's jaw clenched, but he didn't say anything more. Instead, he walked out of the department without looking back.

"Lewis? In my office." Captain Curt Vance's voice was stern.

Garth swallowed a sigh and made his way over to his captain's office. He closed the door and then dropped into the seat across from Vance.

"Care to explain what that was about?"

"Jemma McNally has a no-contact order against Officer Cunningham. There have been a series of incidents that give me reason to treat Cunningham as a possible suspect. Apparently, he doesn't appreciate being under scrutiny."

"Do these incidents include the assault on you?" Vance asked. His captain was short, round, and bald, but he was a fair and decent guy. Garth normally had no issues with his boss.

"Yes, sir. And the most recent slashed tires on Ms. McNally's van."

"I see." Vance drummed his fingers on the desktop. "Okay, then. But I want you to be careful to follow the rules while working on this. I don't want any lawsuits filed against the department."

"Understood." Garth waited a beat, then rose to his feet. "Thank you."

Captain Vance nodded and turned his attention to the mound of paperwork on his desk. Garth surmised his reports were probably buried in there somewhere, yet his boss was clearly up to speed on what was happening.

After leaving Vance's office, he made a quick call to Trina. "Anything going on?"

"Nope. Quiet as a cemetery," she informed him.

He frowned at her choice of words as he strode outside. "Okay, do me a favor and stay there until I arrive."

"Will do."

When he reached The McNallys' B&B, he was glad to see Trina's squad car was parked squarely in front of the house. He pulled off to the side of the garage and waved at her, indicating she shouldn't leave right away.

She rolled down her window. "What's up?"

"I need you to give me a ride back so I can pick up a squad car."

Trina looked pointedly at his truck. "Why?"

He felt the tips of his ears burn. "I'm letting Jemma McNally use my truck while her van is getting repaired."

"I see." The saucy knowing grin on Trina's face made him groan.

"It's not what you're thinking." He slid into the passenger seat. "I'm just giving her a hand."

"Yeah, right," Trina scoffed. "I don't see you going out of your way to let someone like Betty Cromwell use your personal vehicle in a similar circumstance."

Hating to admit she was right, he let it go. "I have names of three of Cunningham's known associates. Two of them are cops, so it's not a stretch to think one of them attacked me."

Trina's expression turned serious. "You're right, it's not a stretch. You want help digging into the backgrounds of these guys?"

"That would be great." He gave her the three names he'd already memorized. "Thanks, Trina."

She shrugged and pulled into the parking lot outside of headquarters. "You'd do the same for me."

"Yeah." That was true. "Keep in touch," he said before getting out of the squad car. He went inside, signed the paperwork, and picked up the keys to the vehicle he normally used.

It wasn't easy being away from Jemma and Trey, even for thirty minutes. He believed Cunningham was long gone from the area, but he didn't feel better until he pulled up in front of the large yellow house.

The minute he got out of the squad car, he heard a shrill scream from the back of the B&B. Without hesitation, he pulled his weapon and ran around to the side of the house overlooking the lakefront.

JEMMA GRABBED Trey and climbed up onto a kitchen chair. The mouse scrambled across the hardwood floor, heading toward the dining area.

"No!" She didn't want the rodent anywhere in her house, but especially not in the dining area or worse, the master suite.

What if this little bugger ran out during breakfast on Saturday morning? Their reputation would be ruined!

"What is it? What's wrong?" Garth shouted through the

window screen. "Are you and Trey okay? Is someone in there?"

"We're fine," she called. "But there's a mouse running loose! I need you to help me catch it!"

"A mouse?" The incredulous tone made her feel bad for making such a fuss. Garth clearly had been worried about her being in danger rather than scared silly. But honestly, was it her fault she didn't like creepy crawlies? Jazz was the tomboy twin, she couldn't help it if she was the girlie one.

"Yes. A mouse. Please hurry!" She clutched Trey closer as they perched on the chair. Could mice crawl up the legs of a chair? She hoped not.

"I need you to unlock the door," Garth pointed out.

Jemma totally forgot that she'd locked all the doors because Randal had been in town. The mouse was huddled in a corner of the room, as if scared to death.

She swallowed hard and gingerly lowered into a crouch. "Hang on, Trey." Placing one hand on the table for support, she gingerly stepped down onto the floor.

The mouse was in the east corner of the dining area, close to the French doors. "I'll open the front door instead, okay?"

"That works."

Mustering her courage, Jemma put her other foot on the floor and made her way through the great room to the front door. She unlocked it, then stepped back, waiting for Garth to come inside.

"Where is it?" he asked, re-holstering his gun.

"In the corner of the dining room." She hitched Trey higher in her arms and followed him into the other room.

"Where?" Garth asked again. He swept out his arm. "I don't see anything."

"What?" Jemma's jaw dropped, and she stared at the area

where she'd last seen the rodent. "He was there, see? He left mouse dirt behind." Disgusting. "Garth, you have to find it. I can't have him running around while my guests are here. And they're arriving tomorrow afternoon!"

Garth planted his hands on his hips, and it took her a minute to register he was dressed in his full uniform. "Okay, I'll take a look around."

She climbed back up on the kitchen chair while he spent the next few minutes searching through the various rooms for the mouse without success. Finally, he returned to the kitchen.

"I'll set a few traps out, see if we can catch him that way." When she opened her mouth, he lifted his palm. "Don't worry about Trey, they have childproof kinds, little boxes that lure mice in but doesn't let them out."

"My guests," she repeated, feeling helpless. "I can't imagine how they'll react if they stumble across him. I can't have him on the loose in here. I just can't!"

"Jemma," Garth's tone softened. "This is a large mansion sitting on the lake away from civilization. People understand that you can't control everything. Besides, you have to realize that where there's one mouse, there could be others. Let me get the traps and we'll go from there. Okay?"

Others? She shuddered at the thought. But what could she do? "Okay, fine."

"Good." Garth let out a heavy sigh and shook his head. "You have no idea what I went through when I heard you scream. I thought you and Trey were in mortal danger."

She bit her lip. "I'm sorry. I just wasn't expecting it—"

"Never mind. I'm just glad you're okay." Garth glanced at Trey. "You want to go to the store with me?"

Trey nodded. "Can we get a puppy?"

Jemma inwardly groaned. Again with the puppy? If she

wasn't allergic to cats, she'd seriously consider one well known for hunting mice.

"No, to get mousetraps," Garth corrected. "You already know your mom can't take care of a puppy right now."

"But I've been good." Trey's lower lip trembled, and Jemma could hardly stand the pathetic expression on her son's face. "I won't be any trouble and neither will the puppy."

"Let's go for a ride," Garth repeated. "Come upstairs with me while I change my clothes."

"No. Don't wanna." Trey sniffled, and big fat tears rolled down his cheeks. "You're mean."

"Enough," Jemma said sharply. "You need to take a time-out. Sit at the kitchen table."

Trey shook his head. She picked him up and plunked him down in the chair. Instantly, he began to wail.

"If you can pull yourself together, you can go with Deputy Lewis to the store." She raised her voice to be heard over his crying. "If not, then you can stay in your room for the next hour. Your choice."

Trey put his head down on the table and continued sobbing. When Garth took a step toward him, she shook her head, warning him away. Trey had been acting out like this on occasion over the past few months, either because he's in his terrible threes stage or because it's his way of coping with the loss of his father and their abrupt move. Likely, both. But she needed to be strong, to set some guidelines, and wanted Garth to support her in that.

Garth reluctantly nodded and headed upstairs to change his clothes. She returned to her cookbook, looking at the roasted pork loin recipe of her grandmother's that she'd decided to make for dinner. Many of her grandma's recipes were Irish, but not all of them. The roasted pork loin happened to be one of her favorites.

The recipe called for garlic, rosemary, and other herbs. Checking the cupboards, she was pleased to see she had everything she needed.

Trey's wails slowly quieted to soft, hiccupping sobs, which were harder to listen to than his loud crying had been. Terrible threes, she reminded herself. The other teachers at school with small children had often mentioned how difficult it was to deal with three-year-olds. And those were kids who hadn't lost their father from divorce and a move. Trey would be four in October, which at the moment seemed really far away.

She pulled several pork loins out of the fridge, turning to face her son when she heard Garth coming down the stairs.

"Trey? Are you finished crying?"

He nodded but didn't look at her.

"Are you sure?" He nodded again, this time raising his tear-streaked face to look at her. "Okay, then." She took a tissue and went over to wipe his face. "Since you're better now, you can go to the store with Deputy Garth."

"'Kay." Trey slid to the ground and ran over toward Garth who lifted her son into his arms.

The two of them looked so natural together, she had to force herself to look away. Garth had been the one to break off from their kiss, remember? Probably because he wasn't interested in a ready-made family.

Despite the fact that he clearly had a way with kids.

"We'll be back shortly," Garth promised.

"Okay." Her smile faded, her chest tight with emotion as they left the house, together. It wasn't healthy to long for something you couldn't have, so she turned back to her grandmother's recipe.

It was a slow cooker meal that would take several hours, so she quickly got to work, keeping a sharp eye out for the mouse that could be hiding somewhere nearby.

She measured the garlic and rosemary, rubbing the spices along the outer portions of the pork loins. Then she browned them in a pan, before transferring them to the slow cooker. When she finished with the pork loins, she began chopping broccoli and cauliflower, seasoning them with dill and setting them aside to cook, later. Lastly, she scrubbed some small red potatoes and set them aside to be cut and broiled.

True to his word, Garth and Trey returned in less than forty-five minutes.

"How many traps did you get?" she asked, eyeing the large bag curiously.

"Six. Figured we'd put four down here, then a couple upstairs to be safe."

The traps were larger than she'd expected, round in shape and dark so you couldn't see inside. Trey kicked off his shoes and ran over to pick up his favorite mini car, the police cruiser.

"You're sure those are safe to use around kids?"

"Absolutely." Garth began setting them up, Trey watching with wide, curious eyes.

She wrinkled her nose and tried to imagine how the mouse had gotten inside in the first place. Maybe a few days ago when Trey had left the French doors open, when she'd caught him heading toward the gazebo.

Garth set up the traps and placed them in various spots around the house. She was horrified at the bits of mouse dirt he'd found and went a little crazy with bleach, cleaning every last nook and cranny.

When that was finished, Garth set up his laptop

computer on the kitchen table. She made herself a cup of tea and watched as he began researching Randal's friends.

"I found it! I found it!" Trey's high-pitched screech had her jumping around in shock.

"What?" Jemma stared in horror as the mouse darted out of her son's discarded shoe and ran straight toward the mousetrap located in the corner. Garth leaped up from his chair, grinning in satisfaction as the rodent instantly disappeared inside.

"We got him!" Garth exclaimed with pride.

"Thank goodness," Jemma said, putting a hand over her racing heart. "One down, and hopefully no more to go."

"Don't worry, if there are others we'll get them."

She didn't want to think about the possibility.

"Yay, the mouse is gone! I want you to be my daddy," Trey said, wrapping his arms around Garth's legs and gazing up at him adoringly.

Panic flashed in Garth's eyes, and Jemma knew in that moment that her gut-instinct had been right all along.

Deputy Garth Lewis had absolutely no desire to get personally involved with her and Trey.

10

Hearing Trey say the word *daddy* was like a knife to his gut. For a moment he'd heard little Sophie's voice, instead of Trey's.

Guilt intermingled with pain over the loss.

Knowing he'd crossed the line of professionalism with Jemma and Trey was one thing, seeing the hero worship in Trey's gaze was something else. He needed, desperately, to find a way to extricate himself from the silken strands of the McNally web.

"I can't be your daddy, Trey," he said, forcing the words past his tight throat. He didn't dare meet Jemma's dark brown gaze. "You already have a daddy."

Trey's expression clouded. "I don't want that daddy, I want a different one. Like you."

Okay, what in the world was he supposed to say in response to that? The thought of Cunningham using his large hands against this small boy was enough to make his stomach churn.

Jemma would never tolerate anything happening to her son, so he forced the image away. Yet he still needed to find a link between Jemma's ex and the series of incidents that transpired here recently.

"Trey, are you ready for a snack?" Jemma offering a treat to her son as an obvious distraction worked. The little boy let go of his legs and turned toward his mom.

"I want a-aminol crackers!"

"Animal," Jemma corrected patiently. She scooped Trey up and plopped him onto his booster seat, studiously avoiding Garth's gaze.

He understood he was overstaying his welcome, but he also didn't want to leave them here, vulnerable and alone.

"Only a few crackers," Jemma was saying. "Dinner will be ready in an hour."

Whatever Jemma was cooking smelled delicious, and he found himself looking forward to the meal.

After a brief internal debate, he took a seat at the kitchen table, returning to his laptop. He decided he'd stay the night as promised, since he had to work in the morning anyway.

Tomorrow Jemma's first guests would arrive, and he wanted to be here when they showed up. Oh, he'd checked out each of the four couples and found nothing out of the ordinary, but he still wanted to be there.

If nothing else, to let them know that law enforcement was close at hand.

He spent more time investigating the two cops, Kevin Rhymes, Cunningham's current partner, and Ben Skubal, his former partner. On the surface, they looked like average cops. Studying their police academy photos, he thought Skubal could possibly look like the guy described by the Pre-K teacher. The hair color was right, although it was cut military short in the photo. But if the guy had grown it out, maybe.

Still, the question remained, why would any cop risk his career to help Cunningham kidnap his son? The obvious answer was that Cunningham had something that he could hold over the head of either his former partner or current partner. Something bad or damaging in some way that could be used as leverage to force the issue.

Garth stared at the two photos for a full five minutes, his thoughts whirling. The former partner? Or current one? He wasn't sure but wondered why Cunningham had been reassigned to a new partner in the first place.

With a sigh, he turned his attention to Cunningham's old college roommate, Peter Dunn. Since Dunn wasn't a cop, he went to social media first, to find a recent picture of the guy.

The photo that bloomed on the screen sent a burst of adrenaline through his system. Dunn had long greasy dirty blond hair and had a vacant look in his eyes, as if he might be on something.

The description was very close, but the fact that the guy was obviously on either drugs or alcohol gave him pause. People with substance abuse issues weren't exactly known to be reliable. Thinking back to the baseball card and the assault on him a few nights ago, it was difficult to imagine someone like Dunn swinging a police baton at his head.

Maybe he just didn't like the idea of being caught off guard by someone like Dunn. He turned the screen toward Jemma.

"Could this guy be the one at Trey's preschool?"

Jemma wiped her hands on her grandmother's apron and came closer. She frowned and nodded. "Maybe. Although, it's hard to say. Isn't that Pete Dunn?"

"Yeah." Garth turned the computer back toward him.

"His last known address is Chicago. I think I'll give him a call, see what he has to say for himself."

"Seems, I don't know, like he's not smart enough to do all this." Jemma waved a hand encompassing the B&B. "Maybe I could see him slashing the tires on my van, but dropping the baseball card? Pretending to be Randal? Assaulting a cop?" She shook her head. "Doesn't seem likely."

"My thoughts exactly. However, don't you think your ex-husband could be smart enough to use several people in his scheme? Maybe once Dunn was nearly caught at the preschool, Cunningham dumped him and moved on to someone else."

Jemma nodded thoughtfully. "You're absolutely right. We may not be looking for one man in particular, but several."

Including Ahern, he thought. Dunn had the first job of kidnapping Trey but failed, so Cunningham approached Ahern and told him to drop the baseball card. It didn't explain Trey's sighting of his father, but maybe the little boy had been distracted by the sailboat, nothing more.

Then came the assault on him, which Garth believed had to have been done by either Rhymes or Skubal since Ahern had been sleeping off his drunken stupor in jail. The slashed tires could have been either of them as well.

Even Cunningham himself, although he doubted it. Easy to see why Cunningham had showed up at headquarters this afternoon. Jemma's ex had wanted to flaunt the fact that he had an alibi for each of the incidents Garth was investigating.

What he needed now was a way to anticipate Cunningham's next move. Unfortunately, his crystal ball wasn't working.

Garth continued to work until Jazz and Dalton arrived

for dinner. He shut the laptop with a click and carried it up to the yellow room to put it away.

At the top of the stairs, he listened to the conversation going on in the kitchen below. He couldn't hear words, just the low murmur of voices and the occasional burst of laughter. Every molecule in his body wanted to go down to join them.

Still, he didn't feel part of the group, no matter how much he wanted to be. This weird longing was ridiculous considering he'd only known the McNally twins for the past four to six weeks, when he'd responded to the threat against Jazz back in April. Yet, he wanted more.

Growing up in the foster system, he'd always been on the outside looking in.

He didn't like feeling that way again now.

"Garth? Hurry up, man, I'm starving, and Jemma won't let us eat without you!"

"Coming!" He headed down the curved staircase, unable to stay away. When he crossed through the great room and joined the three adults and Trey in the kitchen, Garth he felt like he belonged.

Even though he really didn't. And shouldn't.

"We've pretty much finished the master bathroom and bedroom," Jazz was saying. "They were the worst of the areas that needed to be fixed. The rest will take a while. But in the meantime, I thought we'd start working on the garage apartment."

"There's no rush on that," Jemma protested. "Trey and I are fine in the master suite."

"We want to do this," Dalton reassured her. "And better to start the work now, in the summer months than in the winter. In fact, I've already gotten the building permit. We're good to go."

"I can help," Garth offered without thinking. Three sets of adult eyes turned toward him, and he could feel the tips of his ears burning. Was this the proof he needed that he wasn't a part of the group as he'd thought? "What? I can swing a hammer, I'm not helpless."

"Actually, we'd love the help," Dalton said. "The good thing about working in the garage is that we're pretty much starting from scratch. No demo work, we don't even need to raise the roof. We can start adding the studs for walls any time."

Adding studs for walls didn't sound easy, but he could swing a hammer and knew both Jazz and Dalton were renovation experts. They'd done a phenomenal job rehabbing the B&B as well as the old Stevenson place.

"I think it's important for Trey to have his own room, too," Jazz said, smiling at her nephew. "Right, Trey?"

The boy nodded. "It would be better if I had a puppy to share my room wif me. Right, Mom?"

Garth swallowed a groan. It seemed that no matter what they did the idea of a puppy was cemented in Trey's brain.

"Puppy?" Jazz lifted a brow.

"Goldendoodles from a few houses to the west," Garth confirmed.

"I promise to be good," Trey went on. "Puleeze?"

Jemma dropped her chin to her chest in a sign of defeat. "We'll see, Trey. Maybe once we have a place to live that's not here on the main floor of the B and B."

Jazz and Dalton exchanged a look that was difficult to interpret, but he sensed that they were on board with the puppy idea.

He was too. Mostly because it was impossible to resist the little boy's plea. And on a personal note, he remembered wanting a dog while growing up, but the foster families he'd lived with had nixed that idea in a heartbeat.

Even when Doug and Susan Emory had taken him in, Susan's allergies had prevented him from getting a dog.

He knew Jemma wasn't thrilled with the additional work that would come along with a pet. And he felt bad in the role he'd played in exposing her son to the idea.

He could only hope that someday Jemma would forgive him.

THERE WAS no way to win the puppy war, Jemma thought with a heavy sigh. But she could at least put it off until the garage apartment was finished.

A project that could easily take months. And even then, she would need to make sure there was an intercom to the garage apartment so the guests could reach her at any time in the event of an emergency.

After dinner was finished, Jazz, Dalton, and Garth all headed out to the garage. She stayed behind to double-check that she had everything she needed to begin cooking for her guests the following day.

She decided to add strawberry and rhubarb scones to the list, thinking it would be nice to offer their guests something to eat as they arrived. Going through the cabinets, she took note that she was getting low on flour and needed to ask Jazz to pick some up at the store.

Earlier she'd gotten a call from the insurance company on the cost of replacing all four of the van's tires. Wouldn't you know, the total was just under her thousand-dollar deductible.

Cha-ching.

Her simple goal of getting back into yoga had cost her entire savings. Money she'd have to dish out for replacement tires and rims.

Or she could wait a few weeks, until guest money rolled in.

Frustrating. She'd been so determined to regain her independence. To prove she could stand on her own two feet and to run a successful business. But she couldn't deny the veneer of her confidence was starting to crack. While cleaning up the kitchen, and finding no new mouse dirt, thank goodness, she heard loud banging from the garage. Were they at work already? There was no need.

Although, truthfully, she loved the thought of having her own space, away from the B&B. Being on call for their guests was one thing, but having a separate space to call her own was so much better.

Once the kitchen was clean, and she had her ingredients all set out so she could get started with her baking early the next morning, she bathed Trey, then played with him until his eyelids fluttered shut.

She tucked him into bed, her heart full of love for her son.

Seeing the photograph of Peter Dunn had shaken her, badly. Was it possible he was the one? The creep who had almost gotten his grimy hands on Trey. And Garth's theory about Randal using a variety of people to do his dirty work bothered her as well.

Difficult to know where the next threat would come from. And she wasn't naïve enough to think there wouldn't be another attempt.

It was only a matter of time.

The following morning Jemma rose early, anticipation of her arriving guests along with worry that her baking wouldn't be up to par robbing her of the chance to sleep in.

The scent of coffee greeted her as she crossed the dining area. Her steps slowed when she realized Garth was seated at the table, dressed in his brown uniform, cradling a mug in his hands.

"Good morning." It seemed as if days had passed since she last saw him, rather than twelve hours. The sound of hammering stopped at about eight thirty last night, and she'd forced herself to stay in the master suite with Trey.

"Morning." Garth jumped up and turned on the burner beneath the red teakettle. "I helped myself to a bowl of cereal and a bagel, hope you don't mind."

"Of course not," she assured him. "Do you have time for a hot breakfast?"

"No. I need to get an early start." He polished off the rest of his coffee and carried the empty mug to the sink. "Thanks anyway. Oh, what time do you expect your guests to arrive?"

The butterflies in her stomach felt like a flock of giant crows fighting for a way out. "I'm not sure, but check-in starts at three p.m. On our website, we ask people to arrive no later than nine p.m."

"Okay." He tucked his hat beneath his arm. "I'll see you around three."

"Thanks." It was reassuring to know Garth would be there, not that she expected trouble. "Have a good day."

"You, too." He stared at her for a long moment, and she had the insane thought that he might kiss her goodbye, but of course he didn't.

The teakettle let out a shrill whistle, startling her.

"Later," Garth said, heading toward the front door.

"Bye." She took a deep breath and let it out slowly, trying to bring her pulse down to normal levels. Or what passed as normal today, the first day of their new business. Turning back to the counter, she chose an organic green tea bag from her eclectic collection, feeling the need for an extra boost to start the day.

The sound of a buzz saw made her groan. No way, Jazz and Dalton wouldn't start working on the garage again today, of all days, would they?

"Mommy?" Trey's voice was thick with sleep as he padded into the kitchen wearing his superhero jammies. "I'm hungry."

Cold cereal and bagels seemed the way to go, especially since she'd be making a large breakfast tomorrow and Sunday. She picked up her son, nuzzled him for a moment, then set him in his booster chair. "What are you in the mood for? Wheaties or Raisin Bran?"

"Wheaties."

The noise from the garage grew louder as they ate. The sawing in particular began to grate on her nerves. Didn't her twin realize how important today was for them? They needed great guest reviews to get noticed. Offering the gazebo wedding package was a good marketing tool, but no one would care if the reviews related to the accommodations sucked.

She began making her grandmother's strawberry rhubarb scones, doing her best to ignore the noise. Surely, Jazz and Dalton would come in looking for breakfast.

No doubt, they'd be disappointed to find cold cereal and bagels.

"Morning," Jazz said, entering the kitchen.

Jemma rounded on her twin. "What in the world are you doing out there? This is hardly the best day to start working on the garage apartment."

Jazz looked shocked at her outburst. "We have until

three, right? That gives us almost eight hours, plenty of time."

"Are you crazy? Why start today when you can't work on it over the weekend? Our guests are coming for peace and quiet, not the cacophony of saws and hammers." To her utter astonishment, tears pricked her eyes.

"Whoa, Jem, what's wrong?" Jazz hurried over to envelop her in a big hug. "I'm sorry if the noise bothered you. I guess we got a little carried away."

Jemma grabbed onto Jazz, soaking up her twin's strength. "It's not that. I'm a nervous wreck," she confessed. "What if they hate my cooking? What if this first weekend ends up being a huge flop? What if they get bored here without anything to do? What if—"

"Stop right there." Jazz's tone was sharp with exasperation. "First of all, we can't please everyone. Second, you're an amazing cook, so no worries about the food. And lastly, they're here to spend the night and have a good breakfast, it's not our job to entertain them! The town has plenty of boats to rent and other lake activities going on, we don't have to specifically offer things for them to do here. Now I want you to sit down and have another cup of tea."

Jemma clung to her twin for another minute before reluctantly letting go. She collapsed into the closest chair and put her head in her hands.

"You're starting to scare me," Jazz said, placing a mug of tea in front of her. "What brought on all this?"

Jemma took a sip of her tea. "It's been building all week. Between stressing about Randal and the pressure of our opening weekend, I'm losing it."

Jazz glanced at the stuff sitting on the counter. "Do you want me to help?"

That made her laugh. "Um, no. You're far better with a hammer than a spatula."

"Yeah. No joke." Jazz came over to sit beside her. "But honestly, Jem, I don't like seeing you stressed out like this. If it's too much for you, we can hire someone to cook. Maybe we can convince the cook at Daisy's Diner to come work for us."

"No, it's fine." Jemma waved a hand. "I'll be okay. Truly. Just chalk it up to a minor panic attack."

"If you're sure." Jazz glanced around the kitchen. "No need for you to worry about feeding me and Dalton today. We'll grab something at the diner and bring something in for lunch, too. That way you can have the kitchen all to yourself."

"Thanks, Jazz, but you don't have to go to the diner for breakfast. Help yourself to cereal and bagels. Bringing something home for lunch would be great, though."

"Done." Jazz gave her another quick hug, then set about pulling bowls out of the cupboards.

When Jazz and Dalton were finished, they went back to work on the garage. Feeling calmer, Jemma made her strawberry rhubarb scones, then worked on the cranberry muffins.

She taste tested a strawberry rhubarb scone, relieved when it melted in her mouth. Perfect.

The rest of the day dragged slowly. After lunch, she went out to see what Jazz and Dalton were doing in the garage. They had already put in a subfloor and were putting up studs for the interior walls.

As promised, Jazz and Dalton finished working at two thirty and agreed to take Trey for a few hours to keep the boy out of her hair. Garth arrived at three sharp, and their first guests arrived shortly thereafter.

Jemma offered tea, lemonade, and decaf coffee along with the strawberry rhubarb scones. The first couple were in their mid-fifties, Mr. and Mrs. Waylon Perry, who were here to celebrate their thirty-third wedding anniversary.

The rest of the guests arrived within the next ninety minutes, but the engaged couple ended up being just a young woman.

"I'm here alone. My fiancé had to work at the last minute," Sherry Talbot said with an apologetic smile. She was a tall, willowy woman with jet-black straight hair and classically beautiful features that made Jemma feel like a frump.

"Not a problem." Jemma hid her disappointment. "I hope you'll enjoy the blue room. And if you haven't decided on a wedding venue, we have a brochure about our gazebo wedding package."

"Interesting," Sherry said in a noncommittal tone. Jemma's hopes of securing a new wedding weekend dissipated, but she did her best to keep a smile on her face.

After Ms. Talbot left, Garth gently tugged her aside. He'd stayed in the kitchen where he wouldn't be as noticeable but could still see the guests as they checked in.

"Does she look familiar to you?"

She wrinkled her brow. "Who? Sherry Talbot?" When he nodded, she shook her head. "No, why?"

He looked thoughtful for a moment, then shrugged. "Never mind. It's probably just my imagination."

"Well, that's the first hurdle," Jemma said, carrying the tray of empty cups and plates to the kitchen. "Next up, breakfast tomorrow."

A knock at the front door had her turning around in surprise. All four couples, minus one fiancé, had arrived. She wasn't expecting anyone else.

She opened the door to find a well-groomed man with sandy brown hair wearing tan khaki pants and a navy-blue polo shirt standing outside. He was slight in stature but his smile seemed genuine. "Hi, I'm wondering if you have an available room for the night?"

Peering past him, she could see there wasn't anyone else accompanying him. "Sure, please come in." Putting her unease aside, she stepped back to allow him to enter the B&B.

She could feel Garth's gaze boring into her back as she went through the process of obtaining ID and payment for the night.

This was what they wanted, right? To have all their rooms filled with paying guests?

Yet as she took his information, she couldn't help thinking that providing a room to a man traveling alone might be more than she'd bargained for.

11

L istening to Jemma warmly greet the stranger, sweetly informing him of their amenities, grated like nails on a chalkboard. Garth didn't like the fact that this guy would be staying here overnight alone, and the caveman part of him wanted to butt in between them, flashing the gun on his hip, staking his claim.

Jealous? Ridiculous. The guy wouldn't be here more than a day or two at the most. Besides, he had no personal claim on Jemma.

No matter how much he might want one.

Still, he needed to let this guest know that he was armed and on guard. He subtly eased closer to the doorway, hoping the guy would catch a glimpse of him. But the new guest didn't appear to notice, his gaze riveted on Jemma.

Keeping his mouth shut wasn't easy, and one second after Jemma escorted the stranger upstairs to the rose room, Garth went to the desk to get a good look at the guy's driver's license.

His name was Dominic W. Williams, and the driver's license was from Michigan with a Detroit address.

At least he wasn't from Bloomington or Chicago, Illinois.

Garth quickly copied down the name and DL number, so he could run a background check. On the heels of Cunningham showing up in McNally Bay, it was difficult to believe the stranger's arrival was nothing more than a coincidence.

A sense of alarm hit hard. There would be many strangers staying at the B&B each week. How could he run background checks on all of them?

"Five rooms with paying guests!" Jemma exclaimed, breezing into the kitchen. "I'm so excited!"

"Jemma, listen . . ."

"Not now," she cut him off. "I have to bring scones and decaf coffee to Mr. Williams."

He ground his teeth together hard enough to crack a filling. "This is important, Jemma," he tried again. "We don't know anything about this guy."

Ignoring him, she put a couple of scones on a plate, added a cloth napkin, silverware, and a hot cup of coffee with a tiny container of creamer and a bowl of sugar cubes. She lifted the tray and carefully edged past him.

His laptop was in the yellow room, so he followed her through the great room and up the curved staircase. Remembering the layout of the upstairs, he took strong satisfaction in knowing his room was right next to the one where Williams was staying.

The door to the rose room was open. Jemma had set the tray on the bed and was still chatting with her latest guest. Garth scowled and made sure to walk directly past the open door to his room. Even better for this guy to understand there was a cop sleeping next to him.

Garth didn't linger but carried the computer downstairs to the kitchen. It didn't take long for him to access the database and to verify that Dominic Williams didn't have a criminal record.

The only red flag was that the guy was listed as self-employed. He tapped his fingers on the table trying to envision what type of work this guy did that would send him traveling throughout the state staying at B&Bs.

Insurance sales? Some other kind of sales? Travel Agent? Computer software troubleshooter? The more he thought about it the more options he could come up with. He made a mental note to sit near Williams at breakfast the next morning.

Jemma returned to the kitchen and flopped into the chair across from him. "I did it! Everyone is settled in, and Jazz and I don't have anything more to do until early tomorrow morning."

"Yeah, you're a natural, Jemma." His earlier annoyance had evaporated, and he was proud of what she'd accomplished. "I did a background check on Williams, no criminal record. No financial issues either."

Her smile vanished, and she gave him the evil eye. "You can't keep doing this, Garth. You can't screen every guest we have throughout the year."

"I know." He leaned forward, propping his elbows on the table. "But considering what's been going on around here, don't you think this is the best approach? You have no way of knowing if that same guy was the one who slashed your tires because Cunningham asked him to."

She made a *phfft* noise and waved her hand. "He's a nice guy, clean-cut and well mannered. Not the type to slash a woman's tires."

"Yeah, just like Ted Bundy was an all-around great guy." He didn't bother to hide his sarcasm as his frustration began to build. "Jemma, as a single mother you have Trey to protect. You can't afford to be so trusting of strangers."

Her brown eyes darkened, and she jumped to her feet. "How dare you insinuate I'm putting my son in harm's way by running a B and B? I'm the one who called you with concerns over Randal being here, remember? I know very well that I need to be careful. But that doesn't mean I'm going to turn away a paying guest."

Fighting wasn't going to solve anything, so he did his best to corral his emotions. "I'm sorry. I didn't mean to say you weren't being careful. I'm only trying to point out that doing background checks on your guests is a small price to pay for some peace of mind."

"For your peace of mind? Or mine? Frankly, we need the money, or doesn't that matter? Don't you care about what I'm going through?"

"Of course I do." He was puzzled by her sudden outburst. The money reference was probably related to her tires, and he wanted to offer to take care of it but sensed that would only cause her to become more upset.

Jemma abruptly sighed and dropped her chin to her chest. "I'm sorry." She shook her head and looked up at him. "I don't know what my problem is today. I lashed out at Jazz earlier, and now I'm doing the same with you."

He stood and crossed over to her. "I'm sorry, too. I shouldn't add to your stress level on your first official day of business." He drew her close for a brief hug. "Forgive me?"

She buried her face against his chest and nodded. He cradled her close, offering comfort. Her arms crept up around his neck, and the way she clung to him set his blood humming. Being with her like this felt so right.

He liked her and wanted her with a passion he hadn't

felt in years. He knew Trey was temporarily staying with Jazz and Dalton, so he gently lifted Jemma's chin, threaded his fingers through her silky hair, and captured her mouth with his.

JEMMA readily and willingly lost herself in Garth's kiss. He tasted sweet from the strawberry in her scones, and his passion made her blood surge with want and need.

It had been so long since she'd been treated like a lovely desirable woman. And now that she had the sensation within her reach, she never wanted to let it go.

"MOM!" Trey's excited voice, followed by the sound of a door slamming shut, had her pulling abruptly out of Garth's embrace. She took a wobbly step backward and tried to smooth her hair. "Aunty Jazz got a puppy! But I get to name her. I picked Goldie!"

Puppy? Huh? She struggled to pull herself together enough to follow her son's logic. "I told you, we can't have a puppy while there are guests staying here."

"It's our puppy," Jazz said, coming in behind Trey. Her twin lifted an eyebrow and glanced between her and Garth in a way that convinced Jemma that her sister knew exactly what they'd been doing before she'd interrupted. "We're going to keep her at our place, but we're going to share her with Trey."

"Goldie is so pretty, Mom," Trey added, hopping from one foot to the other. "You hav'ta come see her! Hurry!"

"We'll watch the puppy," Jazz reiterated, seeing the skeptical expression in Jemma's eyes. "And Trey will be able to play with Goldie whenever he wants, but we'll do the work."

It seemed too good to be true, and probably was, but she decided it was the best compromise she'd get. "Okay, then, introduce me to Goldie."

Trey grabbed her hand and pulled her toward the door. "You're gonna love her, Mom."

Jemma wasn't so sure, but when the little fluff of blonde curls began running in circles around her, wagging her tail with excitement, she melted.

"Isn't she amazing?" Trey asked, taking the puppy from her arms and holding her against his chest.

"She is." Jemma looked up at Jazz. "Thank you."

Jazz grinned. "She's just here for a visit, she can't be released for another week. But she's ours if we want her."

"I want her," Trey said with a devout expression on his face. "Please?"

"We'll share her," Jazz said, ruffling Trey's hair.

Jemma knew she owed her sister, big time. This was the perfect compromise.

Now she needed to hold up her end of the bargain. How her guests enjoyed her breakfast would be the best indication if their little business would succeed . . .

Or fail.

INWARDLY REELING from the impact of Jemma's kiss, Garth tried to focus on Trey and Jemma interacting with Goldie. He had to give Jazz credit for coming up with the optimal solution to the puppy problem.

His pulse still hadn't settled into a normal rhythm in the aftermath of their kiss, and he wondered if it ever would. His attraction to Jemma was growing stronger each day.

Telling himself he needed to remain professional wasn't working. Even forcing himself to remember Kate and Sophie didn't help.

Somehow, Jemma and Trey had wiggled their way into his heart.

"Okay, Trey. Time for Goldie to go back to her mom," Jazz said.

"Nooo," Trey protested.

"Trey." Jemma's tone held a stern warning. "Aunt Jazz told you that Goldie isn't old enough yet. She still needs her mommy."

"Just like you, do," Garth added. "Come on, Trey."

Trey reluctantly released the puppy into Jazz's care.

"Jemma, we're bringing over dinner tonight," Dalton spoke up. "We'll drive the puppy back and then pick up a couple of large trays of lasagna from the local Italian restaurant. Sound okay?"

"Absolutely," Jemma said with a smile. "Gino's, right? Their food is awesome."

Jazz suddenly snapped her fingers. "Oh, that reminds me! I was thinking we should cross promote, get flyers from Gino's, Chen Lee's, and Daisy's Diner for our guests."

"I'll grab a handful from Gino's tonight," Dalton offered.

"Thanks." Jemma reached for Trey's hand. "Time to get back to the B and B."

Garth swept his gaze over the area as they made the trip back to the house. Nothing seemed out of place, but it occurred to him that it had been almost forty-eight hours since Jemma's tires were slashed. Granted, Cunningham had shown up at headquarters earlier in the day, but Garth still sensed that another attempt against Jemma and/or Trey wasn't too far off.

Stalkers took a perverse pleasure in keeping their victims off balance. He had no reason to believe Cunningham was any different. In fact, just the fact that Cunningham had come here to confront him told Garth a lot.

The guy had showed up to gloat. To prove his innocence when they both knew he was anything but. Based on Garth's expert opinion, he knew Cunningham was paying someone to assist him in stalking Jemma and Trey. If not for the attempt to pick up Trey at his preschool, he'd think her ex only cared about hurting her. But Trey was also in danger, maybe more.

The more he thought about it, the more he grew convinced that Jemma's most recent guest, Dominic Williams, was the guy to watch. Good thing his room was right next door.

If Williams made a move, Garth would be ready.

Their dinner was delicious. Jazz and Jemma's guests left to find their own dinner, and when the nice couple celebrating their thirty-third wedding anniversary came down, exclaiming that something smelled good, Jemma gave them Gino's flyer.

"We need to find a way to offer discounts." Jemma returned to the kitchen table, her expression thoughtful.

"That's a wonderful idea," Jazz chimed in. "I'll make the rounds to the local restaurants tomorrow after breakfast, see if anyone is interested in co-marketing. We can offer a discount here, too, for their guests and vice-versa."

"I like it." Jemma's eyes lit up with excitement. "We're all catering to the same tourist crowd, right?"

"Absolutely," Jazz agreed. "I should have thought of it before. Marketing was supposed to be my thing to do."

"I'm pretty sure you were distracted by a certain hand-some architect," Jemma teased, winking at Dalton.

Garth smiled as the twin sisters continued to plan. He had no doubt that they would make this B&B a success. Especially with Jemma's amazing cooking.

He helped her clean up the kitchen after Dalton and Jazz left. The way Jemma avoided his direct gaze made him wonder if she regretted their kiss.

"Trey?" She wiped her hands on a dishtowel and turned to look for her son. "It's almost bath time."

"I'll finish up here," he told her.

"Thanks." Jemma took Trey's hand and led him into the master suite.

Five minutes later, Jemma's cell phone rang. He looked at the screen, noting a guy by the name Jonas was calling. He hesitated, then quickly answered the call.

"Hello?"

There was a pause. "Who is this?" a male voice demanded.

"Deputy Garth Lewis, I'm answering Jemma's phone. Who are you?"

"Her brother, Jonas." The protectively terse tone didn't change. "Where's my sister?"

"Bathing Trey. If you give me a minute, I'll be happy to get her for you."

"Yeah. I'll wait."

As he'd spoken, Garth made his way from the kitchen, through the dining area tables to the master suite. He rapped on the door, then opened it a crack. "Jemma? The phone is for you."

"You answered my phone?" The sharp edge of her tone indicated she was not happy.

"Yeah, sorry, but I recognized your brother's name on the screen." He held it out to show her. "It's Jonas."

"Jonas?" Her irksome expression faded, and her eyes lit up with excitement. "Come in, Garth. Watch Trey for me, would you?"

He entered the suite and followed the splashing sounds to the bathroom. Trey was surrounded by bubbles, laughing. Garth handed her the phone, and she eagerly grabbed it.

"Jonas? I'm so glad you called! Are you finally coming home?"

Kneeling beside the tub to keep a close eye on Trey, he listed to Jemma's side of the conversation. Her initial excitement morphed into concern.

"The hospital? When? Are you okay?"

He knew Jazz and Jemma had four older brothers, Jeremy, Jonas, Jacob, and Jesse. No clue what their birth order was, but it seemed as if Jonas and Jemma were close.

"Okay, listen. I want you to come here to the B and B the moment you're discharged from the hospital, you hear me? Jazz and I will take good care of you. And there's a VA hospital in Battle Creek Michigan which isn't far from here, so I'm sure we can make it work out."

That didn't sound good. Trey began to shiver, so he decided bath time was over. He picked up a towel. "Time to get out, Trey."

"No," the boy instantly protested. His chattering teeth told a different story, and it didn't take long for the boy to try to stand.

"I've got you." Garth lifted him out and set him on the bath mat. He wrapped the towel around Trey and began rubbing him dry. "Better?"

Trey nodded.

"I'll talk to you soon, Jonas," Jemma said, bringing the conversation with her brother to a close. "Love you."

"Everything okay?"

She gave a tiny shake of her head. "Not really. Jonas was injured in the line of duty but won't tell me specifics about what has happened. Just claims he'll be home within a week or two. Which seems odd, as the government loves to tie everything up in red tape. Makes me wonder if he's been in the hospital for longer than he let on."

"Military?" When she nodded, he asked, "Where was he stationed?"

"Afghanistan." Jemma slid her phone into the back pocket of her jeans. "I'm sorry I snapped at you for answering my phone. It made me think about how Randal used to monitor my calls. But I would have been really upset to have missed Jonas's call."

"No problem." He could tell she was worried about her brother and wished there was something he could do to make it better.

"I'll take over from here." She reached for Trey. "Time to get into your pajamas. Would you like Superman? Or Pokémon?"

"Superman," Trey answered.

Garth retreated from the master suite, giving Jemma and Trey their privacy.

He lingered in the kitchen, but she didn't return. He heard several guests arriving back after being out and realized that even if they were innocent, the fact that Jemma had to leave the door open for them created problems. Randal could easily get in and out while guests were mingling about.

Dominic Williams was the last one to return to the B&B, giving Garth a nod of acknowledgment before heading up the stairs to the rose room. Garth tried to take some satisfaction in the fact that Williams knew a cop was staying there.

He went to his own room to finally change out of his uniform, donning comfy jeans and his police academy sweatshirt. He remained quiet, straining to listen, but couldn't hear Williams moving around.

Either the walls were unusually thick or the guy was tucked in for the night.

He wanted to head back downstairs to be with Jemma but forced himself to stay where he was. Offering her comfort wasn't nearly as important as keeping her safe. That was the lesson he'd learned the hard way with Kate and Sophie.

Better to stay close to Williams, his main suspect. Garth stretched out on his bed and crossed his hands behind his head.

If the guy was innocent, then fine. But he wasn't going to make a mistake.

He dozed on and off for several hours when the creak of a floorboard sent him bolt upright.

Williams!

Garth rushed across the room, pulling open his door, trying to peer through the darkness. Williams's door was open a crack, confirming his suspicions.

The guy was on the move.

Garth grabbed his weapon from the bedside table and descended the stairs, stepping to the far right on the third step from the top, the one that he knew squeaked under a man's weight. His heart thudded when he couldn't see Williams.

Had he lost him?

The sound of a door opening caught his attention, and he quickly moved through the kitchen toward the French doors. There! A dark shadow moved outside toward the lake.

Tightening his grip on the gun, he followed Williams outside. If the guy was up to something, he wouldn't hesitate to stop him.

Using force if necessary.

12

After tossing and turning for what seemed like several nights instead of hours, Jemma slid out of bed and went into the kitchen to make some herbal tea.

Stressing over her upcoming breakfast wasn't going to help. How could she cook a decent meal if she didn't get a good night's sleep?

Seeing the French doors standing ajar brought her to an abrupt halt. Randal? She hurried over to close them in time to hear someone shouting, "Stop! Put your hands where I can see them!"

What in the world? The voice sounded like it belonged to Garth, but she couldn't see the two men outside clearly enough to say for sure. And who else was out there? Randal? She pulled the door open. "Garth? Is that you? Should I call nine one one?"

"Hey, man, what's your problem? Can't a guy stand in the gazebo to make a phone call?"

The second voice definitely didn't sound like Randal's, but still she hesitated. What if the guy out there was someone Randal had hired to harm her? Oh sure, he could say he was just standing in the gazebo to make a phone call, but he was still trespassing on private property.

"I'm calling nine one one now," she said loudly, even though she didn't have her phone handy.

"Go ahead," the strange voice said, sounding exasperated. "Some B an B you're running here, lady. A cop pulls a gun on a guest for no reason."

What? A guest? Jemma felt as if she'd been punched in the stomach. No. Garth wouldn't have followed one of her guests out here, would he? The instant the question formed in her mind she knew the answer.

Of course he would.

"Who's out there?" she asked. "Is that you, Mr. Williams?"

"Get inside, Williams. Now," Garth said in a no-nonsense tone.

"Garth, stop it. You're overreacting." She couldn't believe this was happening. Talk about a public relations nightmare.

The two men came inside. Her guest, Mr. Williams, crossed the threshold first, followed by Garth who still held his service weapon.

What was wrong with Garth? This was insane. She did her best to make amends. "Mr. Williams, I'm so sorry. Please allow me to make it up to you. I'll be happy to give you your money back . . ."

"Not until you tell me what you were doing outside in the middle of the night," Garth interrupted. "This is a B and B, not a hotel."

She wanted to grab Garth and shake some sense into him. This wasn't how you treated a guest! "Stop it, Garth. As a guest he has every right to go outside to the gazebo or down to the lakefront."

"In the middle of the night?" Garth asked.

"Yes." She kept her tone firm.

"Listen, I'm sorry," Dominic Williams said, holding his hands up in a gesture of surrender. "I didn't mean to cause an alarm, but I couldn't sleep. I could see the gazebo from my window and thought listening to the waves would help me relax."

"Why didn't you just open your window?" Garth countered.

"Hey, I wish I had," Dominic said, glaring at Garth, then at his gun. "I didn't know a trigger-happy cop would follow me outside."

"Earlier you said you went outside to make a phone call," Garth challenged. "Which is it? Phone call or couldn't sleep?"

"I, uh, couldn't sleep so I was going to get some air, listen to the waves, and make a phone call." Her guest looked genuinely confused. "Is there a law against that?"

"No, of course not. Garth, I need you to stop, right now." Jemma hoped her tone wasn't loud enough to wake Trey. "Mr. Williams, please accept my sincere apology for what happened here tonight. I'll be happy to refund your payment."

"Hold on, Jemma. You're being stalked by your ex-husband. I think that trumps B and B rules." Garth turned toward her guest. "Frankly, I don't appreciate you sneaking around the house after midnight."

Jemma lifted her gaze to the ceiling, forcing herself to count to ten. She was close to losing her temper in a big way. She only made it to five before stabbing Garth with a steely glare.

"Garth, Mr. Williams doesn't need to know about my personal troubles," she managed between clenched teeth. She turned to her guest. "Again, please accept my sincere apologies. And of course a full refund."

Mr. Williams glanced between her and Garth, then offered a shrug. "I'm sorry, too. I guess I didn't think going outside would be a big deal. I've never stayed in a B and B before, just thought it would be a nice change."

After tonight, Jemma figured the poor guy would likely never try a B&B again. Garth didn't say anything. Maybe he finally figured out just how angry she was at his ridiculous shenanigans.

He'd pulled a gun on her guest! This madness had to stop.

"I'm sorry," she repeated. "Is there something I can get you? Tea? Water?"

"No thanks. I'll, um, just go on up to bed. Good night." Dominic Williams gave Garth a wide berth as he left the kitchen to head back up to the rose room.

The minute she heard the door shut behind him, she rounded on Garth. "What were you thinking?" she asked in a harsh whisper. "The poor man couldn't sleep so you followed him and pointed a gun at him? Have you lost your mind?"

Garth had the grace to look sheepish. "Jemma, listen, I understand you're upset, but you have to admit his going outside after midnight was suspicious. I couldn't let him try to hurt you or Trey."

She stared at him wondering if that bump on his head had caused permanent brain damage. That was the only rational explanation for his behavior. "He didn't try to hurt us, he went outside to listen to the waves. The gazebo and the lakefront is considered public space, and he has every right to use them. Being on the lake is a perk for our business, remember? The view is a big part of why people will come here rather than someplace else."

"That's his side of the story." Garth shrugged. "First it's a phone call, then it's listening to the waves. I'm not so sure I believe either excuse. He could have made a call from his room or opened his window to hear the waves. Honestly? We really have no idea what he was up to."

Shaking her head helplessly, she knew there was no getting through to him. Garth was a cop, he saw the worst in people all the time. And she understood to a point.

But living in fear, suspecting everyone of wrongdoing wasn't the type of life she wanted.

Not for her. Not for Trey.

"I can't do this anymore," she said, overcome with weariness. "You need to leave after breakfast tomorrow."

"Jemma, wait," he said, taking a step toward her.

"No." She backed away from him, wishing his woodsy scent wasn't so compelling. "Enough is enough. That guy might press charges against you! And even if he doesn't, I won't have any guests if you keep pulling stunts like this. I'm going to refund Mr. Williams's money. Hopefully that will make it less likely that he'll slam me with a scathing review or worse."

"Jemma, please . . ."

She shook her head. There was nothing he could say that would make this right. Giving up on the notion of tea, she turned and crossed through the breakfast tables toward the master suite. On the way she detoured long enough to make sure the French doors were locked, before disappearing into her room.

Thankfully, Garth didn't try to stop her.

Despite her anger, she managed to get a few hours of

sleep before she crawled out of bed at five thirty in the morning. Letting Trey sleep in, she quickly showered and changed before going into the kitchen.

After filling the teakettle, setting it to boil and making a large pot of coffee, she did a mental inventory of what she needed to do. She had fresh Irish brown bread for her planned French toast all ready to go. The cranberry muffins still needed to be baked as did the lemon-poppy seed bread. She set about getting those items ready and safely put into the oven before she turned her attention to the full Irish she needed to prepare. Sipping her tea, she opened the fridge to pull out a carton of fresh eggs.

A sound behind her had her whirling around, her heart thumping with adrenalin. She didn't relax when she saw Garth standing there.

"Coffee will be ready soon." She purposefully turned back to what she was doing. She estimated how many eggs she needed for the French Toast batter and began breaking them into a large mixing bowl.

"Thank you." She felt Garth come up beside her. He opened a cupboard and helped himself to a mug, at ease in her kitchen after spending so much time here.

Ignoring him wasn't easy. She whisked her eggs, thinking about the spices she wanted to add. Vanilla and cinnamon for starters. Maybe a pinch of nutmeg.

"I'm sorry," Garth said, breaking into her thoughts. "I'm packed up and will leave after breakfast."

She was upset at what had happened, but her anger had faded to the point she considered backing down on her insistence that he leave the B&B. Only the thought of Mr. Williams giving her an awful review kept her from succumbing to temptation. "That's fine. Now, if you don't mind, I need to concentrate on my menu."

"Okay, I understand." He filled his mug and moved away from the counter.

Risking a quick glance over her shoulder, she noticed he went into the dining area to take a seat, rather than sitting at the kitchen table, the way he normally did. Relieved he was acting as if he was just another guest, she focused on her meal.

Jazz arrived shortly thereafter, pitching in to help serve their guests. An hour later, the first of her guests arrived. It was the couple celebrating their thirty-third wedding anniversary, Mr. and Mrs. Waylon Perry. "Look, honey, isn't the gazebo lovely?" Mrs. Perry said. "What do you think? Would Noelle and her fiancé, Marvin, consider having their wedding here?"

Jemma's ears perked up at the word wedding. Oh, if only she and Jazz could book a few of the wedding packages! She kept busy in the kitchen while listening as Jazz greeted their guests.

"Good morning, Mr. and Mrs. Perry. What would you like to drink? Coffee? Tea? Juice?"

"Coffee," the husband and wife said at the same time. They laughed.

"Coming right up." Jazz entered the kitchen to get their coffee. Jemma wondered how the Perry's managed to stay together for thirty-three years. Her marriage to Randal hadn't lasted more than four.

And that had been three too many.

"Two French toast breakfasts," Jazz said, returning to the kitchen a short time later. "And they're discussing the gazebo as a potential wedding site for their daughter."

"I heard, wouldn't that be amazing?"

"I've already given them a brochure," Jazz confided. She placed two cranberry muffins and two slices of lemon-poppy seed bread out on a plate for them to eat and went back out to the dining room.

Jazz kept her informed as the rest of their guests straggled in, keeping them busy. Even Mr. Williams joined them, ordering the French toast. Jemma hoped he wasn't still holding a grudge and knew she had to let Jazz know about what had transpired during the night. One of the other married couples ordered the full Irish without the blood pudding, so she had two skillets going at once. Sherry Talbot, the woman who'd come alone because her fiancé had to work, joined Mr. Williams at his table and also ordered the full Irish.

At roughly eight thirty, Trey had come out of the master suite, padding over to the kitchen while still wearing his Superman pajamas. She plunked him at the table and gave him something to eat, knowing Jazz would help keep an eye on him.

"That's it, Sis," Jazz said with a relieved sigh. "Everyone is fed and out of the dining room."

Glancing at the clock on the wall, Jemma noted the time to be about ten thirty in the morning. "That's great."

"Oh, and the guy who showed up alone left his key on the table. Sounded as if he was leaving."

Jemma nodded, making a mental note to refund his money. "What about Garth?"

"I'm right here," he said from the doorway.

"Come on, Trey. Let's take a walk, shall we?" Jazz seemed to know she needed a moment alone.

When the door shut behind Jazz and Trey, a heavy silence fell between them.

"I'm sorry about last night," he said, placing his empty coffee cup on the kitchen counter. "Please call if you need anything, okay?"

"I will." She forced a smile. "Everyone finished their meal. I hope that means they liked it."

"It was delicious," he told her. "I heard a lot of praise from your guests. Even Dominic Williams."

She didn't want to rehash everything that had transpired with Mr. Williams. It was all too mortifying. "Yes, well. I have a lot of work to do. My kitchen looks as if it was hit by a tornado. And Jazz and I are splitting the cleaning of the guest rooms."

Garth nodded and moved through the kitchen toward the front door. There was a tiny part of her that wanted to call him back, to give him another chance, but she forced herself to turn away.

Her first breakfast had been a success despite the disaster from the night before. She and Jazz needed to focus on making the B&B profitable.

For her sake and Trey's. Which meant Garth could no longer be a part of the plan.

STRIDING to the squad car he'd left in the driveway, Garth brooded over how badly he'd blown it with Jemma. Why had he gone so far over the edge as to pull a gun on her guest?

Because he didn't trust the guy. And had feared the guy was about to do something to harm Jemma and Trey.

Yet, even he knew that wasn't good enough. As a trained cop he knew better than to jump to conclusions. This was the exact opposite of the mistake he'd made with Kate and Sophie. Two years ago, he'd thought the threat against them had been neutralized, but he'd been wrong.

This time, with Jemma and Trey, he'd imagined a threat that didn't exist.

The guy might file a complaint against him with his boss, but he didn't care. He deserved it. But if Williams took out his anger on the B&B by leaving a scathing review, there was nothing he could do to fix it.

The guy's excuses for going outside on a chilly May evening were lame, but not completely unbelievable. Yet looking back, Garth still couldn't shake the thought that something was off about the guy.

The background checks he'd run hadn't yielded anything suspicious, but that may only mean that Williams hadn't gotten caught yet.

He noticed the woman, Sherry Talbot, who'd come alone for the weekend, walking down the driveway toward the highway. Her long dark hair had been pulled back in a ponytail, and she wore figure-hugging workout gear. Figuring she must be going for a walk, he lifted his hand in a wave as he drove past.

She frowned, as if she didn't recognize him, then returned the wave half-heartedly. As he headed into town, he found himself wishing he'd have gotten Williams's license plate number so he could keep an eye out for the guy's vehicle, in case he decided to stick around McNally Bay for a while.

Paranoid? Maybe. It was a hazard of the job. Cops had to trust their instincts, and his had been jangling the moment the guy had shown up on Jemma's doorstep. Although, to be fair, he wouldn't have even zeroed in on Williams if it wasn't for all the trouble Jemma's ex was causing.

Had Williams truly been up to something last night? Maybe he was planning to call Cunningham, to give an update or to get further instructions. He wished Jemma wouldn't have insisted on refunding the guy's money. At least, not until he knew the guy was innocent.

Garth drove to his apartment building, feeling at loose ends. He'd taken the weekend off so he could keep an eye on Jemma and Trey, but now he decided the best way to do that was to be on the job.

First shift was almost halfway over, but that didn't mean he couldn't pick up some second or third shift hours. When he made the call, Alex readily agreed to give up his graveyard shift.

As the day wore on, Garth realized how lonely he felt without Jemma and Trey. In the short time that he'd become involved with them, they'd filled the gaping hole in his life.

He'd felt the same way about Kate and Sophie, too. And looked how that turned out? His lapse in judgement had caused Kate's ex-husband to find them. It was a minor miracle that Kate and Sophie had survived.

But his relationship with them had never recovered. Kate had lost faith in his abilities to keep her and Sophie safe. She'd informed him that she'd decided to move with Sophie back down to Florida to live with her mother. He'd offered to move with her, but Kate had refused. She'd told him she needed time alone, but he knew that was just a polite way of saying their relationship was over. Not just over, but disintegrated beyond repair. Dead and buried.

The last time he'd seen her, she and Sophie had left the hospital bandaged and bruised as they made their way to a rental car he'd obtained on their behalf. Once they were settled inside, Kate had driven away without once looking back.

The guilt of the near miss had haunted him for the past twenty-four months. And here he was, making the same mistake all over again with Jemma and Trey.

Apparently, he had a knack for destroying potential relationships. Time to accept the fact that he was destined to live alone.

By dinnertime, he decided to walk over to Daisy's Diner. The food wasn't nearly as good as Jemma's, but it was decent and familiar. Yet when he entered the diner, he didn't feel the same sense of home that he used to.

Ashley was working and greeted him with a warm smile. "Hey, Garth, how are you?"

"Good, Ashley." The place was busy, so he gestured to the one empty seat at the counter, way off in the corner. "Is that spot open?"

"Absolutely." She waved him over, then filled a water glass for him. "I assume you don't need a menu?"

"Nah. I'll have a burger with the works."

"Sounds good." Ashley crossed over to the register and put his order in.

Garth turned sideways on his stool, putting his back against the wall so he could sweep his gaze over the patrons of the restaurant. As it was a Saturday evening, he saw far more strangers than regulars, likely tourists. It occurred to him that Jemma and Jazz had picked a good time to open their B&B. May was the start of the tourist season, and by June they would be overrun by visitors.

His gaze stumbled across a woman seated in a booth. She was studying the menu with her head down, but he was fairly sure the woman was Sherry Talbot. Not that her eating dinner here was unusual, but it was still a bit jarring to see her here.

It was hard to imagine what a woman on her own would do to pass time in McNally Bay. I mean, sure, they had boats for rent, and fishing was big. Their main street was quaint, but half the shops weren't open yet. The Cozy Quilt shop was open, maybe Sherry was interested in that. Or maybe she had a secret passion for fishing.

He inwardly shrugged. What Sherry Talbot chose to do with her time was none of his business. He was hardly the expert on female hobbies.

His burger arrived ten minutes later, and he dug into his meal with gusto. Glancing at his watch, he estimated he had five hours before he needed to report in at 11:00 p.m. for his shift.

Feeling better about the fact that he could at least watch the McNally Mansion from afar, he dawdled over his food. The burger was medium rare and the fries extra crispy, just the way he liked them.

What were Jemma and Trey having for dinner? Were they right now sharing a meal with Jazz and Dalton?

Stop it. He wasn't a part of their group. Being the outsider looking in was something he should be used to by now.

"Would you like dessert?" Ashley asked, refilling his coffee cup.

"Not today, thanks. Just bring me the bill."

"Here you go. Hope to see you again, soon." Ashley gave him a friendly pat on his arm as she left.

After settling his bill, he stood to leave. As he turned back to face the restaurant, he saw that Sherry Talbot was still in her booth. Which wouldn't have been that unusual except that she wasn't alone.

He abruptly stopped in his tracks, the tiny hairs on the back of his neck lifting in alarm. Dominic Williams was seated across from Sherry. Not only had the guy not left town, but he was in a deep discussion with Sherry that made it seem as if they knew each other as more than passing acquaintances.

Garth quickly turned and recaptured his seat. He gestured for Ashely. "I changed my mind about dessert," he told her.

"Great! One slice of apple pie coming right up."

Garth nodded, then surreptitiously glanced over his shoulder. It didn't appear as if Sherry and Dominic had noticed him.

He told himself there were plenty of reasons the two had ended up here, together. It's a small town. They were both here alone. An innocent coincidence.

But deep down, he didn't believe it.

13

J
emma cleaned the kitchen, a task that helped burn off her frustration, then turned her attention to cleaning the two remaining guest rooms. Jazz had done four of them and then had taken Trey to visit Goldie the puppy. Since the rose room and yellow rooms needed to be fully cleaned, she threw herself into the work, stripping the beds and putting the towels and linens in the washing machine. Then she scrubbed down the two bathrooms, finding a strange sense of satisfaction in making the tile and chrome sparkle.

She'd skipped lunch. But now her stomach was growling. Glancing at the clock, she realized it was almost dinnertime. Finished with working for the day, she walked to the house next door to see how things were going with Jazz, Dalton, and Trey.

Goldie was still playing with Trey, and Jemma couldn't deny how adorable the Goldendoodle was. Lifting the puppy to her face, nuzzling the soft skin, made the last vestiges of stress melt away.

"You love her, Mom, don't you?" Trey asked.

"I can't deny it." She looked up at her sister. "I really appreciate you doing this."

"Hey, it will be fun for both of us. Shared responsibility, right?" Jazz laughed.

Jemma nodded, then sighed, giving Goldie back to Trey. "I need to fill you in on what happened last night."

"What do you mean?" Jazz looked confused, then her gaze narrowed. "Did you hear from Randal?"

"No, no." She waved a hand. "Nothing like that. Actually, things have been quiet on that front, and I'm hoping to keep it that way."

"Then what is it?"

Jemma grimaced. "Garth went a little crazy." She went on to fill her twin in on everything that had transpired.

"He pulled a gun on a guest?" Jazz echoed in horror. "I can't believe it! What on earth was he thinking?"

"He was thinking the guy was going to hurt Jemma or Trey," Dalton said, sticking up for Garth. "Why wouldn't he be on high alert? It's suspicious to go outside to hear the waves in the gazebo after midnight if you ask me."

Since that was exactly what Garth said, she couldn't argue. "Maybe, but I felt terrible and refunded his money." She glanced at Jazz, hoping her twin wouldn't be upset. "It was the only way I could think of to prevent him from hitting us with a lousy review. And even then, there's no guarantee. He may still leave one anyway."

"Yeah, I get that." Jazz shook her head. "But it's really a bummer. Not a stellar debut, huh?"

"No. Although, you thought breakfast went well." Jemma tried to focus on the bright side.

"It did. They raved about the food, Jemma. Truly." Jazz reached over and gave her a quick hug. "Don't worry about it, okay?"

"I'll try," Jemma agreed. "Mr. Williams was only staying the one night, so tonight should be a breeze." She paused, then added, "I kicked Garth out."

Jazz's jaw dropped, and she exchanged a worried look with Dalton. "Sis, are you sure that was a good idea?"

"Jazz, think about it. What am I supposed to do? Have Garth follow every guest who goes outside at night because they can't sleep? He already chased away one potential guest, I can't afford to let him do that with another."

"Yeah, but . . ." Jazz's voice trailed off. "I don't know, Jem. I wouldn't care one way or the other if it wasn't for Randal."

"Nothing has happened since the tire incident." Jemma wasn't sure why she felt the need to defend her decision. She was tired of worrying about Randal. She'd thought Jazz would be on her side on this, not on Garth's. "I don't want anything else to go wrong. From what I overheard of their conversation with you, it seemed like Mr. and Mrs. Perry might encourage their daughter to hold her wedding here. That would be huge for our business."

"That's true." Jazz smiled. "They did seem interested in the idea."

"Do you want me to stay in Garth's room for tonight?" Dalton offered. "Having another man around couldn't hurt."

"That's sweet, but you and Jazz are right next door. I'll be fine." She watched Goldie and Trey play, her son giggling as the puppy licked his face. Why the sudden flash of guilt over the way she'd treated Garth? No clue. But she needed to get over it already. "Oh, I almost forgot. I heard from Jonas last night."

"You did? Is he coming home?" Jazz asked. "I'd love to plan our wedding if he is."

Jemma lifted a hand. "Hold on. Yes, he's coming home, but he's also been injured. He called from the hospital."

"Injured? How? What happened?"

"He wouldn't give me the details," Jemma told her. "But it sounds like it's bad enough that they'll be sending him stateside, but not bad enough that he couldn't talk. That's encouraging, don't you think?"

"Yeah, I guess." Jazz glanced at Dalton, taking his hand. "It's good he'll be home soon."

"Yes, it is." Jemma wished her brother would have been a bit more forthcoming with the details of his injury. They were quiet for a moment, lost in their thoughts. Jemma knew that as much as she and Jazz had wanted Jonas to come home, this wasn't what they'd been hoping for. "Anyway," she said, changing the subject. "I thought I'd make something easy for dinner, hamburgers and brats. Are you okay with that?"

"Absolutely," Jazz agreed. "I nominate Dalton to do the grilling."

"Hey, you didn't even give me a chance to offer my excellent grilling services," he protested. "Give me a little credit here. I'm happy to do my part."

Jazz's response was to lean in for a quick kiss. Jemma smiled, happy that her twin had found her perfect match with Dalton O'Brien. It hadn't been an easy road, they'd both had to learn to trust and to love again. But seeing them together made all the tough stuff worth the effort.

When Garth had kissed her—was that just a day ago?—she'd thought that he might be someone she could lean on. Someone she could trust. Love.

Her heart squeezed painfully in her chest. *Love?* How had that happened? She hadn't realized how she'd allowed her fantasy surrounding Garth's becoming a permanent part of hers and Trey's life to gain momentum.

Until she'd forced him to leave. She swallowed hard,

overcome with a sense of sadness. Ridiculous to pine over schoolgirl fantasies.

For her, that level of happiness and togetherness just wasn't meant to be.

G ARTH HAD BARELY TAKEN three bites of his apple pie, when he noticed Sherry and Dominic had gotten up to leave. He tossed money on the counter to cover his dessert and tip, then slowly eased off his stool. He wanted to follow without being too obvious.

He paused just inside the doorway leading out of the diner, watching through the window. Surprisingly, Sherry and Dominic didn't embrace or kiss but barely spoke as they went their separate ways.

Sherry walked in the direction of the grocery store, while Dominic got into a charcoal gray sedan. When Williams exited the parking lot, he drove in the opposite direction from Sherry.

Moving quickly, Garth headed to his squad car, wishing he had his personal vehicle rather than one announcing he was a cop. But he'd left his truck for Jemma to use, and she was so furious with him, the last thing he wanted to do was to renege on their deal.

He made sure there were a couple of cars between them as he followed Williams out of town. Was the guy leaving after all? There was a part of him that had wondered if Sherry and Dominic had planned a secret rendezvous. Were they both cheating on their spouse or partner? It would explain why she'd showed up alone, followed shortly by Dominic's solo and unexpected arrival.

Had Dominic planned on meeting Sherry in the gazebo?

If so, why? Wouldn't it have been better to liaison in his room or hers? And if they were seeing each other on the sly, they didn't show it at the diner.

None of it made any sense, but his gut was screaming at him that there was something wrong with this picture.

He lost track of Williams's charcoal gray sedan, but then found it again a few miles later. Breathing out a sigh of relief, he tried to increase his speed in an attempt not to lose him.

The blue interstate sign caught his attention. Garth lifted his eyes in surprise. Apparently, Williams was leaving Clark County, heading back to Detroit.

Except, he wasn't. Garth's pulse kicked up a notch when Williams took the westbound ramp off the interstate, not the eastbound one. The westbound would take him through Indiana toward Chicago, not Detroit.

Weird. Maybe the guy was some sort of salesman and had more business to do. On a Saturday? Possibly. Or maybe he had an appointment lined up in the Chicago area for Monday? Could be the guy wasn't headed to Chicago at all, but somewhere else entirely. Garth followed Williams onto the freeway for a good ten miles before he finally turned around to return to Clark County.

He should be relieved Williams was gone and not coming back. But as he drove back toward McNally Bay, he realized that this only proved that Jemma was right.

He was an idiot. A crazy man who'd pulled a gun on her guest for no good reason. His actions had forced her to refund his money, taking a bite out of her desperately needed income.

Okay, it was only one night, not an entire weekend, but still, Jemma had every right to be concerned. If Williams decided to slam her with a horrible review, other guests may choose to go elsewhere. There were other hotels and B&Bs in the area, not to mention new ways to secure travel accommodations. Airbnbs were all the rage, and people could get an entire house for dirt cheap. The prices didn't include breakfast, but for some people that wasn't a problem. The houses came equipped with kitchens so guests could make their own meals.

His stomach knotted as the magnitude of what he'd done sank deep. He'd been so sure Williams had been hired by Cunningham to cause harm to Jemma and Trey. But he'd been wrong.

In fact, Garth had been the one to hurt them.

He returned to his apartment to kill more time before he needed to shower and dress for his shift. He managed to get two hours of sleep, but that only ended up making him feel groggy rather than refreshed.

Drinking a large mug of coffee helped. He reported in to work, sipping another mug of coffee as he listened to the update provided by the previous shift, summarizing the events that had gone down during the day.

"We broke up a party on the lakefront near shift change," one of the deputies said. "I'd recommend swinging by again because it's a Saturday night and they could easily go back to the same spot, or a different one."

Garth nodded, knowing that was exactly what a group of bored teenagers might do. "Anything else?"

"There's a suspected meth lab not far from the Pine Cone Campsite." The deputy shrugged. "We've been trying to catch someone in the act to give us a reason to bust in there, but so far, they've been keeping a low profile. I'd swing by every couple of hours, keep them on their toes."

"Any idea who owns the place?" Garth asked.

"A guy out of Chicago, Kevin Worth."

The name meant nothing to Garth, and judging by the blank looks on some of the other deputies' faces, he could tell they didn't recognize it either. Unfortunately, illegal drugs were everywhere, even in quaint small towns like McNally Bay.

"The rest of our calls were related to petty crime and the occasional drunk and disorderly, nothing serious. But you get the privilege of being on during a Saturday night bar closing." The deputy smirked. "Good luck with that."

"Yeah, thanks." Garth was no stranger to working third shift on Friday or Saturday nights. Fights tended to break out between drunk patrons any time after midnight and before the bar closed at 2:00 a.m.

Between the bar fights, the meth house, and the kids trying to party on the lakefront, he hoped he'd find enough time to swing by the McNally Mansion.

Cunningham was a cop, so he'd know what a typical Saturday night was like in a small town. If he was planning to make a move, Garth firmly believed it would be sometime around bar time.

But that was okay. He planned to be ready—for *anything*.

AFTER DINNER, Jemma did prep work for the following day, getting banana bread batter and blueberry muffins ready so they could be easily baked first thing in the morning. When that was finished, she took stock of her inventory, making notes of what she'd need to replace before next weekend's guests arrived.

"Trey?" She peered into the dining area for her son. "Ready for bath time?"

"Yep." Trey abandoned his toy cars to run over to her. "I want Garf to help me."

"Deputy Lewis," she automatically corrected, taken aback by her son's request. How was it possible that he'd gotten attached to Garth in such a short time? "Sorry, honey, but he's not here. I think he might be working tonight."

"Cause he's a policeman!" Trey bobbed his head. "Right, Mom?"

"Right." She forced a smile. "Give me a minute to start the water, you pick out which jammies you want to wear."

"Pokémon," Trey announced as they entered the master suite. He ran over to the side of the dresser that contained his clothing. "Mom! Where's my badge?"

"I don't know. Where did you leave it?" She plugged the tub and started the water, testing with her elbow to make sure it wasn't too hot.

"Mom!" Trey's voice raised in alarm. "It's losted! I losted my police badge!"

She suppressed a sigh and returned to the bedroom. "We'll look for it after your bath, okay?"

His lower lip trembled. "I wanna wear it to bed."

She knelt beside her son. "Trey, if we can't find it, I'm sure Deputy Lewis will give you another one. Don't worry about it, okay?" Then an idea hit her. "Were you wearing it when you were playing with Goldie?"

"Maybe." He scrunched up his face. "I don't remember."

"We'll find it tomorrow. Now, time to get into the tub."

Trey did as she told him, crisis averted for the moment. She was tempted to call Garth, to let him know that Trey might need a replacement badge, but talked herself out of it.

If she were honest, she'd admit calling him was just an excuse to hear his voice. Ridiculous at how she'd missed having him around during the day.

Better that she learn how to stand on her own two feet. Leaving Randal had been a huge step in regaining a level of independence. No sense in giving it up now.

After bath time was over, she read Trey a story, but when that was finished, he went back to whining about his missing deputy's badge. Resigned, she placed a call to her sister. Jazz promised to look but called back fifteen minutes later, saying she hadn't found it. Jemma began searching one last time through the B&B, but once again came up empty.

"I want my badge!" Trey cried.

"Shh," she admonished him. "We have guests!"

Trey threw himself onto the bed, sobbing into his pillow. Jemma watched him, wondering where on earth he'd left it. The stupid badge could be anywhere, especially outside, but she wasn't going to search for it in the darkness. Plenty of time to do that in the morning.

Trey grew more and more fussy until finally, a solid hour past his usual bedtime, he fell asleep. Jemma sat on the edge of the bed and dropped her head in her hands with a sense of relief.

Exhausted from the early start and all the drama in the middle of the night, she fell into a restless slumber. Twice she woke up to strange noises, likely from her guests moving around upstairs, but forced herself to stay in bed.

At five thirty she got up, feeling a little more refreshed than she had the day before. This was how it was supposed to be. She left Trey where he was, sound asleep, hoping he'd wake up in a better mood. Making a mental note to reach out to Garth about a replacement badge, she hurried into the kitchen and went to work.

The meal preparations went smoothly, and she found herself getting into a rhythm with Jazz. As the day before, Mr. and Mrs. Perry arrived first. Jazz chatted with them, taking out two mugs of coffee along with creamer and sugar, remembering their preferences from yesterday.

"What will you have? French toast or the full Irish?" Jazz asked.

"We're doing the full Irish today," Mr. Perry announced. "Although I must say, I sincerely doubt that it can top the brown bread French toast."

"I'll pass on your compliment to the cook," Jazz promised. In the kitchen, Jemma felt her cheeks flush with pride. "I guess you'll have to tell me which one you prefer," Jazz continued. "Two full Irish breakfasts coming up."

"Told you they loved your cooking," Jazz said when she returned to the kitchen.

"Here, take the banana bread and blueberry muffins out to them." Jemma pushed two plates toward her sister. "And maybe mention how you're planning to get married in the gazebo this summer, too."

"Great idea," Jazz said. She delivered the plates of baked goods. Jemma listened to her sister, marveling at how natural she was in talking to their guests. "Please let us know if you're really interested in the gazebo wedding package. I'm planning to get married there myself soon."

"Really? Oh, how nice." Mrs. Perry gushed. "I'm going to suggest this venue to my daughter, Noelle. She really wants a small wedding, and I think this setting would be perfect."

Yes, Jemma thought, doing a mental fist pump. Granted, Noelle may have a different idea of where she wanted to get married, but the interest in the gazebo package was promising.

She continued cooking in the kitchen, this time relaxed enough that she could clean up as she went along. Jazz chatted with the guests as they arrived, taking their orders. It seemed that everyone who ordered French toast the day before went with the Irish, and vice versa. Jemma took that as a good sign, as she set up her dueling skillets.

When all the guest breakfasts had been served, she took a moment to sip her lukewarm tea. She and Jazz had determined their check-out time would be 11:00 a.m., and it was only nine forty-five now.

Little over an hour to go, she thought with satisfaction. She was pleased by how well her breakfasts seemed to have been received. What a difference it made having gotten a decent night's sleep with no extra drama.

She picked up her phone, wondering if it was too early to call Garth about replacing Trey's badge, then set it back down again. She'd wait until her guests had all left for the day.

With breakfast finished, she waited for their guests to check out. The Perrys left first, with the other two couples following about thirty minutes later. When they were gone, Jemma returned to the kitchen, she collapsed into a chair.

She'd done it! Survived her first weekend. Then she suddenly frowned, glancing around the kitchen.

Where was Trey?

"Honey? Are you hungry?" She entered the master suite, expecting to find him in the large bed maybe watching television, but he was nowhere to be found.

Panic squeezed her heart, and she spun around to go back into the kitchen. Jazz must have taken Trey to her place once the meals were finished. That's what she'd done the day before. She grabbed her phone and called her sister. "You have Trey, don't you?"

"What? No, sorry, Jemma. I thought he was with you. Why, do you need me to watch him for a bit?"

She tightened her grip on the phone. "He's not there?

Are you sure? He's not in his room, and I don't remember seeing him."

"We'll be right over," Jazz said.

Jemma put the phone down with a shaky hand. How was it that she'd missed seeing her son? What kind of mother was she? Had he decided to go off on his own? To search for the missing badge? Or maybe to see the puppy?

Then it hit her. She didn't remember Jazz giving her a breakfast order for Sherry Talbot either. Jemma bolted upstairs to the green room, searching for her missing guest.

The green room was empty, except for the key that was sitting on the bedside table.

No luggage. No Sherry Talbot. No Trey.

Her stomach knotted painfully as she put two and two together. Instantly, she called Garth, but his phone went straight to voice mail.

Clattering down the stairs, she dialed 911. "Clark County Sheriff's Department, what's your emergency?"

"My son, Trey McNally, is missing. He's almost four years old, and the last I know he was wearing his Pokémon pajamas."

"I'll dispatch a deputy to your location," the calm voice said.

Jemma lifted dead eyes as Jazz and Dalton came in through the front door. "We looked around outside but haven't seen him. I'm so sorry, sis. What can we do?"

Jemma's eyes filled with tears as she helplessly shook her head. "I don't know. I'm afraid Randal has him."

14

Garth woke up to a loud pounding on his apartment door. "Huh?" He slid out of bed and staggered across the room. Pressing one bleary eye to the peephole, he scowled. "Who's there?"

"It's Dalton! Come on, get moving! Trey is gone, and Jemma is a wreck. We need all the help we can get."

The news cleared the cobwebs from his brain in one fell swoop. He yanked the door open. "Trey's missing? When?"

"We're not sure. But that's not all, one of Jemma's guests, a woman by the name of Sherry Talbot didn't show for breakfast either. It's possible the two incidents are related."

The image of Sherry Talbot meeting with Dominic Williams at Daisy's Diner flashed in his mind. "I knew there was something fishy going on with her and the other guy, Williams."

"Come on, man. Put some pants on. We gotta go."

Garth was already on his way to the bedroom. "I'll send a BOLO alert for both Talbot's and Williams's cars. I can get every sheriff's deputy and the authorities in neighboring counties to be on the lookout for them both. Jemma has their vehicle information, right?"

"I think so." Dalton glanced at his watch. "One of the deputies has already been out to the B and B to take Jemma's statement, but they're at a loss as to where to begin searching for him. We've already swept the grounds of both properties and the home of the puppies. But we came up with zilch."

Garth's stomach clenched. How long had Trey been missing? What if Talbot had already handed the boy over to Cunningham? He yanked on his clothes and joined Dalton. "Let's go. I'll follow in my squad car. We may need to split up."

Dalton's response was to head back outside toward his car, leaving Garth to catch up.

When he pulled into the driveway of the B&B, Jemma ran out to greet him. She threw herself into his arms. "My baby. You need to help find my baby!"

"I know." He crushed her close, wishing more than ever he'd done things different. "We'll find him."

"How?" She pulled out of his arms and raked her fingers through her disheveled hair. "Where?"

"Get me the car information on Talbot and Williams. I want to put out an alert."

She didn't hesitate and turned to go inside the house. He followed, his mind whirling with possibilities.

"Here." She thrust the information she'd taken from her guests upon check-in. He was relieved she'd collected vehicle information, including license plate numbers.

He returned to his squad car to issue a BOLO for both vehicles, then began to work the computer. After typing in the tag number for Williams's car, he discovered it was a rental. His hopes plummeted when he got the same results for Talbot's vehicle.

Two rentals leading to dead ends. He should have done an in-depth vehicle investigation on Friday instead of just focusing on the people themselves. If he'd have known they were both driving rental cars, then maybe things would have played out differently.

But it was too late to change the past.

Digging into who rented the cars wasn't easy, each company requested a warrant before releasing what they deemed *private information*. Garth feared that simply having suspicions about the two individuals wouldn't be enough. And he was right. His boss, Captain Curt Vance, initially flat-out refused his request. It wasn't until Garth explained how he'd seen the two suspects together at the diner and how the woman disappeared the same time Trey went missing that he was able to convince his captain to go for the warrant.

"I'll send the information as soon as I have it," Vance promised.

"Thanks." Garth signed off, then looked up as Jemma approached. Her tear-ravaged face stabbed deep, and he hated knowing he'd failed her.

Failed Trey.

The idea of the poor kid suffering at the hands of Williams, Talbot, or worse, his father, made his blood boil and his stomach churn.

"I never should have asked you to leave." Her voice was husky with fear. "Trey would still be here right now if I hadn't kicked you out."

"Don't say that." He slid out from the driver's side and pulled her close. "She may have still found a way to take him."

"No, she would never have gotten past you." Jemma sniffled loudly. "It's my fault. I lost track of him. Lost track of her."

"Stop it." His tone was forceful. "This isn't anyone's fault other than your ex-husband's. I want you and Jazz to keep searching the two properties. I'm going to follow up on whatever information we can get from the two rental companies."

"Two rental companies?" Jemma echoed in confusion.

He filled her in on how he'd seen Talbot and Williams together at the diner. "Both cars are rentals. It's possible they were using fake IDs."

"They were working together?" Jemma looked appalled at the idea. "That's crazy. How could Randal make them do something like this?"

"I'm not sure. He must have something on them." There was something off about the whole mess, and he was angry with himself for missing the clues.

His radio squawked, and he reluctantly let her go to get the call. "Lewis."

"The information you requested has been sent over," Captain Vance said. "Appears both vehicles were rented by the same guy, David Graves."

The name meant nothing to him. "I need any and all known associates of the guy. There has to be some sort of connection to Cunningham. We need to put out a BOLO for this David Graves guy and Cunningham."

"Cunningham, too?" The Captain's tone was full of doubt. "He'll argue harassment."

"Too bad. His kid is missing, and he's the prime suspect." Garth didn't care if the sheriff's department was sued or not, Trey's safety was his only priority.

"Okay," his boss agreed after a long pause. "I'll send them through."

"Good. I'll contact Lieutenant Young, find out if Cunningham reported in to work today." Garth made the call but only reached Young's voice mail. Realizing it was Sunday and the Lieutenant was likely off duty, he hung up without leaving a message.

Jemma's phone rang, and she pounced on it. "Hello? Trey?"

The color drained from her face, and her panicked gaze latched onto his. In that moment he knew whoever was on the other end of the line had her son.

JEMMA COULD HARDLY HEAR the male voice on the other end of the phone through the roaring in her ears.

"Are you with the cop?"

She pulled herself together with a Herculean effort. The caller had to be Randal, but there was something off about his voice. Was he trying to disguise it? "No. Are you with Trey? I want to talk to my son!"

"Don't lie to me," the voice said. "I know that cop has been staying with you. Tell me the truth or I'll hang up right now."

She took a steadying breath, knowing she had to be calm for Trey's sake. "No, I'm not with the cop, I kicked him out last night." She felt Garth's gaze on her as she uttered the lie. "But I did call nine one one and reported Trey missing, so the cops are likely looking for you."

"Then I guess you'd better hurry. If you want to see the kid again."

"You want me to meet up with you?" She didn't hesitate

even though she still couldn't be one hundred percent sure that the caller was Randal. "I'll come right now. Where?"

"I need you to come alone. If I see the cop, or anyone from the sheriff's department, I'll disappear and you'll never see Trey again."

No. Please. She couldn't stand it. "I'll come alone," she rashly promised, avoiding Garth's gaze. "Tell me where you want to meet."

"I'm at the Pine Cone Campsite, in area twenty-three." There was a brief pause. "I'm warning you, Jemma. One hint of your cop buddy or anyone else from the Sheriff's Department and I'm gone."

"I believe you. I'll be there. But—I have to drive Jazz's truck because my van has four flat tires and hasn't been repaired yet."

"What kind of truck?"

She glanced at Garth, who subtly shook his head. For some reason he didn't want her using his vehicle. "Jazz drives a cherry red pick-up truck."

"Fine. No cops, or you'll regret it." The man on the other end of the phone disconnected from the call.

"I need Jazz's keys." She glanced around frantically, relieved when Dalton tossed them to her. She grabbed them, the panic she'd managed to hold at bay returning full force. "Thanks. I have to go, alone."

"Jemma, you can't do this. I need to be there."

"No!" She tried to sidestep him. "You don't understand. I'm not even sure the caller was Randal. It may be one of his friends. And if so, that means Randal could be spying from somewhere close by and will know if I disobey him. I can't risk him taking Trey or worse, hurting him."

Garth lightly grasped her by the shoulders. "Jemma, listen to me. I know the Pine Cone Campsite better than he does. I'll be there. You won't see me and neither will he."

She shook her head, battling a wave of helplessness. "Please, don't."

He tightened his grip on her upper arms. "I need you to trust me."

How could she? How could she trust anyone with Trey's life? Tears pricked her eyes. She knew Randal. The man was a monster, and she feared Garth and the others may underestimate him.

But then again, if she had trusted Garth's instincts on Friday night, Randal or whomever he sent may not have gotten to her son. She reluctantly nodded. "Fine, but if anything happens to Trey . . ." She couldn't finish the thought.

"I know." Garth released her. "He won't see me."

"Where's the campground?" It hit her that she'd never been there.

"Just off highway ZZ. It's on the right, or north side of the street."

She'd find it. She headed over to the driveway next door, where Jazz had left her truck. Moments later she was heading west on highway ZZ.

The signs to the Pine Cone Campsite were easy to see. But once she was inside, the site markings were difficult to find. Some were on one side of the dirt road, and some were on the other, seemingly at random.

She abruptly came upon site number twenty-three. The area was fairly open, not a lot of places for anyone to hide. There also wasn't a tent, only a large black cargo van. The thought that Trey may be stuck inside the back of the van had her heart thumping wildly in her chest.

Sliding out of the driver's side seat, she put her hands up

in the air and cautiously approached along the passenger side of the van. "Hello? Is anyone here? I've come alone as promised."

For several seconds there was no sound, no movement, then suddenly a man stepped out from the front of the cargo van holding a gun in his hand. He was dressed in jeans and a T-shirt that stretched tightly over his chest. She stared in horror as she realized the guy wasn't Randal. It was Stephan Ahern! "Stop right there and get inside the back," he ordered. "Hurry!"

Reeling from the fact that her ex-husband could still be out there, somewhere, she did her best to remain calm. Her instincts were screaming at her to stay out in the open. "No, Stephan. Not until I see Trey. I need to know he's all right."

Ahern sneered. "I'm the one calling the shots here. You took my son, so it's only fair that you understand what it's like to be without yours."

Her stomach knotted painfully as she realized she was dealing with a seriously unbalanced man. All this because she reported Daniel's abuse? She could hardly wrap her mind around it. But Trey was the only thing that mattered. "Stephan, if you don't show me Trey, then I'm leaving. You could have already hurt or killed him."

Ahern stared at her for a long moment before gesturing toward the cargo van with his gun. "Open the back door of the van."

With trepidation, she stepped forward and pulled on the handle. The door swung open, and she could see Trey curled up in a ball, still wearing his Pokémon pajamas. Several baseball cards were scattered around him.

"Mommy?" His tear-streaked face ravaged her heart. "The lady said she was taking me to see Goldie, but she brought me here instead." His lower lip trembled, and his eyes filled with fresh tears. "I wanna go home."

"I know you do." Her relief in finding him unharmed was short-lived. She turned back to Ahern. "I'll go with you, but I want you to leave Trey here. You're upset with me, right, Stephan? I'm the one who caused you to lose your son, no one else. This is just between the two of us. Leave the child out of it."

Surprisingly, Ahern appeared to consider her request. But then he shook his head. "Nope. I don't think you understand what I've been going through. What my life has been like since you took my son away from me." The wild look in his eyes made her fear he wouldn't hesitate to shoot her. "Your son has only been missing for a few hours, I haven't seen Danny in five months."

"I know, Stephan, and I'm sorry about that." She tried to stay focused on Ahern but couldn't help wondering if Randal was lurking somewhere nearby. "Let's talk about it . . ."

"No!" Ahern waved the gun, and she froze, fearing the worst. "Get in the van. Now!"

Jemma hesitated, knowing that getting into this van was the absolute worst thing she could do.

Was there another option? For the life of her she couldn't figure it out if there was. She had the feeling that Ahern didn't want to hurt them here in the campground but would take them someplace else to do his dirty work. Hoping that Garth would follow the cargo van, she took a step forward and lifted her foot to rest on the bumper so she could jump inside.

She heard a shout. "Drop your weapon!" She threw herself inside the van, covering Trey's body with hers. A gunshot echoed through the clearing. Her heart jammed in her throat and she wondered if Ahern had managed to kill Garth.

Then there was nothing but silence.

"Jemma? Trey? Are you okay?"

"Garth?" Moving off Trey's body, she turned to look back. Garth had come around the van from the same side Ahern had been standing and was reaching inside for her. "How? What?" She couldn't pull a coherent sentence together.

"It's all over." He helped her out of the van, then reached for Trey. "Don't look back, okay, buddy? We're going to head over this way."

Despite Garth's directive, Jemma couldn't resist glancing over her shoulder. Ahern was lying on the ground, not moving. His chest was awash with blood, and his gun had fallen out of his hand.

"Randal might be somewhere nearby," she said fearfully.

"He's not, don't worry. Come with me, Jemma."

She tore her gaze away from the dead man lying on the ground. Stephan Ahern had been the one behind everything that she'd blamed on Randal.

And now he was dead.

She couldn't suppress a shiver. Deep down, she'd hoped Randal had been the kidnapper. That he'd end up in jail, forever.

But she'd been wrong. With a sigh, she realized that it was her own fears that had kept her focused on her exhusband as the man behind all the incidents. Which meant she'd have to figure out how to live with the idea that Randal would be free to live his life.

And worse, may once again attempt to sue for joint custody.

∾

"ARE YOU UPSET WITH ME?" Garth asked, pulling her away from the image of Stephan Ahern. As soon as he'd arrived at the campsite, he'd remembered seeing Sherry Talbot hiding behind the tree the morning he'd arrested Ahern. The man with her must have been Williams, aka David Graves. He thought it was possible that Graves had also been the same guy who attempted to pick up Trey from his preschool.

All this time, he and Jemma had assumed Randal was the guilty one. He stood protectively in front of the dead body, unwilling to cause Jemma or Trey to have nightmares.

"He didn't listen when I told him to drop his weapon and I worried if I didn't take the shot the moment you moved out of the way to jump inside the van, he'd fire at you."

"I'm not upset with you." She flashed a watery smile and stepped closer to his warmth. "Thank you for saving us. I'm glad you didn't let me come alone."

"Never." Garth was holding Trey with one arm but pulled her close with the other. He lightly pressed a kiss to her temple, willing his heart to return to normal. "I'm sorry, but Ahern was clearly unbalanced."

Jemma leaned back to look up at him. "I owe you—so much."

"No." He tightened his arm around her shoulders, knowing that most of this was his fault. He'd handled things badly, not exactly the way he had with Kate and Sophie, but the outcome had nearly been the same. "I'm just glad that I was able to get here, this time."

"This time?" She frowned, confusion shadowing her gaze. "What do you mean?"

"There was another woman and child who I promised to keep safe. Unfortunately, her ex got to her. I was too late to prevent the crash." He shook his head, wondering if the guilt would ever go away. "They survived, but not because of anything I did."

"I see. This is your way of making up for whatever mistakes you feel you made in the past? Is that the real motivation here?" Disappointment shimmered in her tone.

"That was the original plan." He closed his eyes and buried his face against her hair. "Unfortunately, I became too emotionally involved. And as a result, I almost failed you."

"No. I'm the one who lost faith in you." She rested her head against his shoulder. Her voice dropping to a whisper. "I should never have doubted you, Garth. Never. You knew something was up with Williams, but I didn't listen."

"I could have handled things better," he countered. "Don't let me off the hook that easily."

There was a long silence, before she whispered, "It seems so crazy that Stephan Ahern would go to such lengths to get back at me. All this time, I thought for sure Randal was the one . . ."

He tightened his hold on her, never wanting to let go. "I know. I did the same thing. But looking back, I think Cunningham came here not just to complain but to size up the situation. He knows we're watching over you. I don't think he'll be much of a threat anymore."

"Maybe not, but he never loved me."

He hated hearing the self-doubt in her tone. "Jemma, he doesn't know anything about true love. If I had a wife and son like you and Trey, I would love and cherish you for the rest of my life."

"Oh, Garth, that's the sweetest thing anyone has ever said to me." Her voice was muffled against his shirt. "Will you please take us home?"

There was so much more he wanted to say, but he held

his tongue. The deputies would need their statements, but no reason they couldn't find them at the B&B. He caught Trina's gaze and gestured her over.

"I'm taking them to the B and B."

"You can't just leave after . . ." Trina's voice trailed off as she realized Trey was listening. "I need to take your statement."

"Take it now or catch up with me at the B and B. Your choice." His tone didn't allow for an argument.

"Now," Trina agreed.

After handing Trey over to Jemma, he walked a short distance away so they couldn't overhear. The last thing he wanted was for Trey to understand he'd shot a man. Garth started with his suspicions about Talbot and Williams, how they'd both been seen together at Daisy's Diner and had obtained rental cars that were paid for by David Graves. "It seems Graves is engaged to Sherry Talbot and Talbot is also Ahern's sister. If you look closely you'll see the resemblance. The three of them got together and decided to torment Jemma, making her pay for ruining Ahern's life. I bet you'll find the cargo van was leased by Graves, too."

"Go on," Trina encouraged.

He explained about Ahern's call to Jemma and the threats. "He held a gun on them, and I feared for their lives. When Jemma moved to get into the back of the van, I had a clear shot. I ordered him to drop his gun, he didn't comply so I fired."

"You didn't give him a chance to surrender?"

"No. Time was of the essence. He was close to escaping with Jemma and Trey. He ignored my command leaving me no choice but to stop him."

She stared at him for a long moment, and he knew what

she was thinking. Every officer involved shooting was dissected under a microscope. But he didn't care.

Given the same exact set of circumstances, he'd handle it the same way.

"Trina, the guy was standing five feet from Jemma with a gun in his hand. He was clearly mentally unstable, and even a lousy marksman could hit the target at that distance. He kidnapped a child, that has to work in my favor."

"Okay, fine." Trina slapped her notebook shut. "I'm sure you'll be hearing from Captain Vance, and you know there will be a full investigation."

"I know the rules." He turned toward Jemma and Trey. "I'll be at the B and B if Vance wants to find me."

He drove Jemma and Trey back in his truck, telling Dalton that he'd drive him over to pick up Jazz's vehicle later. Jazz surprised him by throwing her arms around his neck and giving him a huge hug.

"Thank you for saving my sister and nephew."

"Anytime." He awkwardly patted her back.

"Don't let her chase you away, you hear me?" Jazz stared deep into his eyes. "Jemma needs you. And so does Trey."

He nodded, his heart swelling with hope. Apparently, he was close to being considered as one of the family. At least in Jazz's eyes.

But Jemma was the only one who mattered. And he knew that the real source of her anxiety, Randal Cunningham, was still out there.

An hour later his captain arrived to hear Jemma's and Trey's side of the story. When they'd finished, Captain Vance pulled Garth aside. "We picked up Talbot. She confessed to helping her brother, Stephan Ahern, teach Jemma McNally a lesson about how it felt to lose custody of a child. She also admitted that David Graves, was using the name Dominic

Williams as an alias. She's willing to snitch on both her brother and her fiancée to save her own hide, so that's good. But we haven't found Graves yet."

"I'm sure he's hiding out somewhere," Garth said. "Once he realizes Ahern is dead, they may turn themselves in."

"We'll get him, one way or the other. Although you know this also means we have to apologize to that jerk, Cunningham."

"Yeah, I guess so." Garth didn't like it but understood the need given the way things had turned out.

Vance clapped him on the back. "Good shooting."

"Uh, thank you, sir." Guess that meant he wasn't going to be found guilty of reckless homicide.

"I'll put in a good word for you when they start the investigation."

He nodded. "Appreciate it."

Over the next couple of hours, Jazz and Dalton did their best to create a sense of normalcy. When Trey began asking about the puppy, they agreed to take him for a visit. Garth knew this was their way of leaving him and Jemma alone, yet he couldn't help thinking the timing could have been better. Jemma probably needed time to assimilate everything that had happened.

"Let's go outside," Jemma said, tugging him by the hand toward the gazebo. "I want to watch the lake for a bit."

The gazebo offered a spectacular view of the lake. He slipped his arm around her waist and held her close. For several long moments they simply stood in silence, listening to the waves.

"I've wasted so much time, Garth," she said, breaking the silence. "Running from Randal, being afraid. Never looking to the future. All this time, it wasn't Randal at all, but Stephan Ahern. It makes me realize how much I've let

Randal get to me. Get inside my head. I need to stop thinking and worrying about him."

"I'm sure it won't be easy," Garth said in a low voice. "But you're strong, Jemma. More courageous than you've given yourself credit for. And your ex is smart enough to know that you're surrounded by friends, one of which is a cop and family here. He'll stay away, I'm sure."

She nodded. "Even though Randal wasn't involved, I still feel better. As if I really can do this. Be independent and run a successful business." She tilted her head to the side so she could look at him. "And you know what? A big part of that is because of you."

He tightened his grip, afraid she'd slip away. "I promised to keep you safe, and it bothers me that I almost failed."

"Stop looking at the dark side. You did save us, and that's what matters."

Tough to argue that one. He rested his cheek against her hair. "I've been alone for a long time, Jemma. But I don't want to live that way any longer. I love you. I know it might be too soon for you, and that's okay, but I want you to know how much I love you. If you give me a chance, I promise to love and cherish you and Trey for the rest of my life."

"Oh, Garth." She turned in his arms so they were facing each other. "I'm glad to hear that, because I love you, too. So much that it scares me."

"Love should never be scary," he said with a frown. "I can wait, give you however much time you need. I know this wasn't a good time, trust me, there's no rush."

She cupped her palm against his cheek. "Poor choice of words. I'm not afraid of you, Garth. It's just all this emotion is so overwhelming. I guess there's a tiny part of me that's afraid it's nothing but a dream."

"A good dream," he said with a smile. He lowered his

mouth to capture hers in a heartfelt kiss. When they could breathe again, he went on to add, "The best dream. I've always wanted a big family. Are you okay with that?"

She laughed. "Absolutely. A few kids and a Goldendoodle, right?"

"Right." He couldn't think of anything more perfect.

EPILOGUE

Three weeks later...

Jemma couldn't believe how quickly Garth had woven himself into the fabric of her and Trey's life. Her son loved Garth and looked up to him, rarely asking about his other daddy who, as Garth had predicted, had stayed away from McNally Bay.

A week after the incident, the authorities had arrested David Graves for his role in Trey's kidnapping. Both David and Sherry Talbot insisted they had no idea Ahern had a gun or that he would actually harm the little boy, so the judge had let them out on bail. But Garth had put together a tight case, so she was certain they'd all do jail time.

As long as they stayed far away from McNally Bay, she didn't care what happened to them.

The mystery of Lucy's identity was still unsolved because Mrs. Cromwell had ended up in the hospital before Jemma could meet with her. Thankfully, Mrs. Cromwell was doing better and should be released soon. Rumor had it that Mayor Banks had become a permanent fixture in her hospital room, which made Jemma smile.

Jonas was due home by the end of the week, so Jazz and Dalton had scheduled their wedding for the following weekend. Jazz would be a June bride. Her twin agreed to let Jemma post pictures of the event on their website for marketing purposes. And best of all, they had their first wedding booked! Mr. and Mrs. Perry had confirmed their daughter Noelle would marry Marvin Anderson here in the gazebo at the B&B the last weekend in August.

Each day brought more guests. With Garth at her side, she couldn't ask for anything better.

"Is Trey asleep?" Garth asked.

"Yes, finally." She smiled and wiped her hands on her grandmother's rosebud apron. "One good thing about Goldie, she wears him out."

He smiled, nodded, and held out his hand. "Walk with me."

She took off her grandma's apron, then took his hand, allowing him to tug her outside, past the gazebo toward the lakefront.

She loved his romantic gestures. Not only was he great with Trey, but he always made her feel loved and cared for. So different than what she'd experienced with Randal. Outside, the June weather was balmy and peaceful, a faint breeze causing ripples across the water. The sun was just beginning to set on the horizon, the sky glowing with orange, pink, and purple rays of color.

"It's so beautiful," she whispered.

"You are," he agreed, making her smile.

At the rocky shoreline, he gently turned her around to face him. Then he shocked her by going down on one knee and holding up an engagement ring.

"Jemma McNally, will you please marry me?" He hesitated, then added, "It doesn't have to be this year if that's too soon. Any time in the future would work."

That made her laugh, and she tugged on his hand until he was standing so she could throw her arms around him. "Yes, Garth. Yes, I'll marry you. And it can be this year, if you like. I'm pretty sure Trey would like you to become his step-daddy sooner than later."

"I'd like that, too." He crushed her close and kissed her. When they came up for air, he slipped the ring on the third finger of her left hand. "I love you both so much."

"I love you, too." She sighed and shook her head, gazing at the modest yet beautiful engagement ring that fit perfectly. "Let me guess. Jazz helped you pick out the size."

"Yep." He grinned and threw his arm around her shoulders. "Your sister also told me not to let you push me away. Aren't you glad I listened to her infinite wisdom?"

"Yes." She rested her head on his shoulder and watched as the sun made its final decent behind the lake. She couldn't imagine what she'd done to deserve a second chance at love with Garth, but she wasn't about to let him go.

He was hers, now and forever.

Want to read Jonas and Bella's story next? Click here!

Dear Reader,

I hope you're enjoying my McNally Series. Thank you for all the wonderful notes and emails, you have no idea how authors love hearing from our readers!

Reviews are very important to authors, so if you enjoyed *To Cherish*, please leave a review at the platform from where you purchased the story. Also, if you want to be kept up to date on my newest releases, please stop by my website at www.laurascottbooks.com to sign up for my newsletter. I offer a free novella from my Crystal Lake Series *Starting Over* to all newsletter subscribers. Don't miss your chance to read this heartwarming story.

Lastly, if you are interested in seeing a sneak peek at the next book in the series, *To Laugh*, I've included the first chapter for you to read, here.

SINCERELY,

Laura Scott

Made in the USA
Coppell, TX
29 November 2024

41337229R00111